Trapped!

We took a couple of steps across the frozen dirt floor of the barn when the powerful wind slammed the door shut behind us.

"Ohh!" I let out a startled cry.

All four of us spun around, terrified. The wind howled.

"No one there. Just the wind," Shannon said, sounding very relieved.

We stared at the door. We pushed it open again, until it stuck in the hard, frozen snow.

My heart was pounding. I felt cold all over. I don't think I ever knew what "chilled to the bone" meant until that moment.

Behind us the wind blew hard against the open barn door. I stepped close to Doug, close enough to see that even he looked scared.

We were just about in the center of the barn, our boots crunching loudly on the hard ground. Something fluttered above our heads.

"A bat?" I whispered.

"It isn't a butterfly," he cracked.

When I looked back down, I saw a figure looming just in front of us: a man standing against a post, staring at us.

"He's got a gun!" Red cried.

Books by R. L. Stine

Fear Street: THE NEW GIRL
Fear Street: THE SURPRISE PARTY
Fear Street: THE OVERNIGHT
Fear Street: MISSING
Fear Street: THE WRONG NUMBER
Fear Street: THE SLEEPWALKER
Fear Street: HAUNTED
Fear Street: HALLOWEEN PARTY
Fear Street: THE STEPSISTER
Fear Street: SKI WEEKEND

HOW I BROKE UP WITH ERNIE
PHONE CALLS
CURTAINS

Available from ARCHWAY Paperbacks

FEAR STREET®

Ski Weekend

R. L. STINE

AN ARCHWAY PAPERBACK
Published by POCKET BOOKS
New York   London   Toronto   Sydney   Tokyo   Singapore

AN ARCHWAY PAPERBACK *Original*

An Archway Paperback published by
POCKET BOOKS, a division of Simon & Schuster
1230 Avenue of the Americas, New York, NY 10020

ISBN: 0-671-72480-0

First Archway Paperback printing January 1991

10 9 8 7 6 5 4 3 2 1

FEAR STREET is a registered trademark of Parachute Press, Inc.

AN ARCHWAY PAPERBACK and colophon are registered trademarks of Simon & Schuster.

Cover art by Bill Schmidt

Printed in the U.S.A.

IL 6+

chapter

1

"Doug—slow down!" I cried, closing my eyes as we skidded over the icy road.

"Hey—I can handle it."

Doug spun the wheel and somehow managed to straighten the car out before we slid off the road. Then, before we were even out of the skid, he stomped on the gas pedal and we roared forward again.

"Doug—" I called from the backseat.

He was laughing. He loved scaring us. He loved the danger of it.

Mainly, he loved showing off.

"Ariel is right," Shannon said, sitting beside him in the old Plymouth, sounding frightened. "You're going too fast. You know you can't see two feet in front of your face."

Doug sped up in response. His dark eyes lit up with excitement, and he had a wide grin on his face.

"Tell him to go faster," I told Shannon. "Then maybe he'll slow down."

"Why don't you let me drive for a while," Red said, leaning forward from the seat beside me. He'd been awfully quiet, I realized, ever since we left the ski lodge. "I've driven in snow like this a lot."

"Hey—sit back and leave the driving to us!" Doug said, laughing as if he'd just cracked a hilarious joke. He turned to Shannon. "Stop grabbing my arm, will you? You want to have an accident?"

"Doug—you're really scaring us," Shannon said angrily. She had her knees up against the glove compartment, her arms crossed tightly in front of her.

"You want to get home by tonight, don't you?" Doug said, turning the wheel hard as the car went into another slide.

"Yeah. Of course," Shannon said quietly. Her parents hadn't wanted her to go on this ski trip, but she had begged and pleaded and promised them everything would be fine, and they had finally agreed. She was desperate to get back before they really started to worry and get angry.

Shannon's mom and dad didn't exactly approve of Doug. So she hadn't told them he was going on the trip. If they found out she'd sneaked away with him for a ski weekend, they'd approve of him even less!

"It sure is coming down," Red said, rubbing the steam off his window with a bare hand so he could see out.

There wasn't much to see. It was snowing so hard, the *air* was white!

At least that's the way it looked to me, staring out through the smeared glass.

It had been snowing lightly when we left the ski lodge, little wet flakes that didn't look like they'd amount to much. Then, as we curved down the mountain, the wind began to roar and gust, and the snow began to drop in what appeared to be solid waves of white.

Doug's old Plymouth pitched forward, sliding on each twist in the narrow road. Every time the tires skidded, my heart jumped.

A short while before we took off, a lot of cars had left the lodge on the narrow, winding road down the mountain. But now ours seemed to be the only one in sight.

The wipers made a loud scraping noise as they swept across the windshield. Ice was forming on the glass. I knew Doug couldn't see a thing. So why wouldn't he slow down?

Because he was Doug. Because he loved being Mr. Macho, Mr. Dangerous. I'd known Doug for a long time. He was a really good friend. But that day was one day that I wished Doug weren't Doug!

It would have been so much nicer to have a *sane* person driving!

Scraping across the glass, the windshield wipers did their best, but the snow came down so fast the windshield was constantly blanketed. The wind howled at us, pushing the car roughly from side to side.

My long, straight blond hair had fallen out from

3

under my wool cap. I tucked it back in, then scooted down in the seat and tried to see the late afternoon sky. No way. The falling snow was just too thick and heavy.

It reminded me of a dumb joke of my dad's. He'd pick up a blank piece of paper and say, "Ariel, do you like my drawing?"

"What drawing?" I'd always ask.

"It's a polar bear in a snowstorm," he'd say. Or "It's a snowman at the North Pole." I used to think it was pretty funny. But now that I was in a scene that looked a lot like that blank sheet of paper, it wasn't funny at all.

The tires suddenly whirred beneath us. I uttered a quiet gasp.

"Chill out," Doug said. I guess my gasp wasn't as quiet as I'd thought. "I can handle it."

"Can't you drive with *two* hands?" Shannon pleaded.

"Hey—what for? I need one hand for you," Doug teased, reaching out with his right hand and squeezing Shannon's shoulder.

"Doug—please! You're going to kill us all!"

"Shannon—give me a break, will you?"

The atmosphere in the car was really tense. Partly because we were heading blindly down a mountain on a slick, twisting road with a madman at the wheel. And partly because Randy wasn't with us, and everyone knew I was upset about that.

And partly because we were sharing the car with a stranger, someone we'd only known for a couple of

4

days. Don't get me wrong. We all liked Red right from the start. But it's hard not to feel uncomfortable with someone new around, especially in such a tense situation.

I glanced over at Red, who was staring out his window, his forehead pressed against the glass. "I don't believe this," he said quietly.

Red was really nice, I had to admit. I mean, he'd been especially nice to me ever since we'd met a few days before at the ski lodge. And I thought he was kind of cute with his wavy red hair and intense, dark eyes. But I wished it were my boyfriend, Randy, sitting there instead of this stranger.

Randy.

Just thinking about him made me angry again.

On Thursday afternoon Doug, Shannon, Randy, and I had driven all the way up to Pineview Lodge for a long weekend of skiing and fun, and mainly just to get away from Shadyside. Then Randy had to go and ruin it all.

Thinking about it, I still didn't feel that the fight we had was my fault. I mean, we had planned this weekend for so long. What right did Randy have to suddenly insist we all drive back early on Sunday so he wouldn't miss his stupid basketball game?

If we went back early, we'd lose a whole day of skiing. Staying at Pineview was pretty expensive, and the rest of us wanted to stay and get our money's worth. Naturally, Doug and Shannon disappeared, leaving Randy and me at the little table in the crowded lounge to argue it out.

I couldn't help it. The argument quickly became a screaming fight. People were staring at us, but I didn't care. I mean, Randy is always pulling some selfish stunt like that. I was determined that this one time I wasn't going to give in.

When he said, "Ariel, try to see it from my point of view," I just lost it. I guess I was shouting pretty loud. And that's when he jumped up, knocking his chair over with a loud clatter and drawing gasps and cries of surprise from the four girls at the next table, and stomped out of the lounge.

"I'm not the stubborn one!" I yelled after him. I knew he couldn't hear me, but I wanted to get the last word in.

Then I realized that everyone was focused on me, and I felt really embarrassed. I just sat there staring down at that little table. I didn't get up or anything. I don't even remember what I was thinking.

That was when Red had come over. "Is there anything I can do?" he asked.

I glanced up at him suspiciously, trying to see if he was coming on to me. He wasn't. He looked so cute with that boyish face and all his freckles. He was genuinely trying to be nice.

He sat down and we started talking. He told me he had grown up near these mountains but hadn't been back for a while. He tried to cheer me up, and I took an immediate liking to him.

There are certain people like that, I think. People you meet and right away you know you're going to like them. So when Shannon and Doug came back, I introduced them to Red, and the four of us went into the restaurant to have dinner.

Red hung out with us for the rest of the weekend. Randy had left a note at the front desk saying he was taking the bus back to Shadyside.

The note made me so angry, I tore it into little pieces. I realized Randy probably thought he was a great guy because he bothered to leave a note. Well, I was determined to have a good time without him. And with Red around, having a good time wasn't so difficult. So when he said he needed a ride to Brockton, we were more than happy to help him out.

But now here we were just an hour from the ski lodge, nowhere near Brockton, in the worst snowstorm I'd ever been in, with at least another six hours in the car ahead of us. And I was really feeling bummed out knowing that Randy was home safe and sound, the pig, and probably not even worrying about me for one second.

"It's freezing in here," Shannon groaned, turning to look at me as she pulled the hood of her ski jacket up over her coppery hair. Shannon always looks kind of sad and pouty. That's her natural expression.

But now she looked downright miserable.

"What can I do? Stop and buy a new car? The heater's busted," Doug said angrily.

"Can you see anything at all?" Red asked suddenly, leaning forward into the front seat.

"Yeah. I can see snow," Doug said and laughed at his own stupid joke.

We're never going to make it, I thought glumly.

Then I scolded myself for being such a pessimist. But I can't help it. I'm basically a worrier. I can find something to worry about in any situation. And when I get in a really bad situation like this, I can find *plenty* to worry about.

The car suddenly started to slide. Really fast.

I screamed and gripped the back of the front seat.

Even through the hurtling snow I could see a sheer dropoff to the valley below on our right. And I could see that there were no guardrails along the side of the road.

"No!"

Shannon screamed too.

Doug turned the wheel rapidly in the direction we were skidding. He pumped the brakes, but the car didn't slow.

We're going over the edge, I thought.

We're going to slide right over the side.

I closed my eyes, but it didn't help. I could still feel the slide of the car—and then a sickening pull as we started to spin.

chapter

2

I couldn't breathe. I couldn't utter a sound. I opened my eyes.

The car spun all the way around once. Then it stopped, its front tires wedged in a snowdrift on the side of the road.

Doug had a grin on his face. "Like to see that again?" he joked.

"Uh—Ariel," Red said softly.

"What?" I had actually forgotten that Red was sitting there beside me.

"Uh—Ariel, do you think you could get your hand off my leg?"

I gasped. I was gripping Red's leg so tightly, I must've been hurting him. And I hadn't even realized I was doing it.

I jerked my hand away, feeling very embarrassed,

feeling my face grow hot. I knew I was blushing bright red.

Shannon and Doug laughed and turned around to look at us.

"You've got to watch Ariel. She's very aggressive," Shannon told Red, still laughing.

Big laughs, at my expense. They were all feeling relieved that we were still alive, that we hadn't slid off the road and over the cliff.

But we had very little reason to be relieved, as far as I was concerned. We still had a couple hundred miles to go. And the snow was coming down even harder now.

"Go back. Go back." That's what I imagined the howling wind to be saying. I've got a real imagination, especially when it comes to frightening myself.

Doug backed the car onto the road. I closed my eyes as he did it. The back window was completely covered with snow. I knew he was backing up blindly.

The car chugged, hesitated, chugged again, then started to move. "All *right!* Home, James!" Doug cried happily.

"Can't you do *anything* about the heater?" Shannon asked, shivering. "It's blowing cold air."

"Try putting it on defrost," Red suggested, leaning forward into the front seat.

"It *is* on defrost," Doug said a little edgily. "It's just busted, that's all."

"We're *all* busted," Red said, sounding glum for the first time since we'd met him.

"Well, turn it off then," Shannon said angrily,

fumbling with the controls. "Why do we need cold air blowing on us? It's already twenty below zero!"

"Okay. Fine." Doug impatiently pushed her hand away and slid the heater control to off.

I could see that things were getting tense again up in the front seat, so I tried to change the subject. "Did you know that snow has ten times the volume of rain? That means every inch of rain is equal to ten inches of snow."

Scientific facts like that always distracted me from things that were bothering me. But of course, I'm a science freak.

My companions didn't seem to be terribly interested. Doug groaned loudly and started to tap out a rhythm on the dashboard with his right hand, steering with his left.

"Gee whiz, tell us another one, Mr. Wizard!" Red said, laughing that funny, high-pitched laugh he had.

"Hey—don't make fun of Ariel," Shannon said, coming to my defense. "Someday she's going to be a great doctor."

If we live through this storm, I added to myself, feeling the car slide again, feeling that sense of dread run through my entire body.

What's the scientific explanation for that feeling? I wondered. That creepy feeling you get when you're not sure just how frightened you should be. You start to feel heavy all over, as if you're not going to be able to move, not going to be able to take another breath.

A powerful gust of wind shook the car. "Want me to drive for a while?" Red asked again.

"You got a license?" Doug asked. It sounded more like a challenge than a question.

"Yeah. Sure," Red said calmly. "I'm real good with cars."

"Well—maybe later," Doug said.

"I think we should turn back," I said, staring out at the falling snow.

"Huh?" Doug reacted with disbelief. "Have you lost it totally?"

"We can't!" Shannon cried. "If I don't get home tonight, I'll be grounded for the rest of my life!"

"We've come too far to head back," Red said, turning to me. "We've been driving over an hour. Even if we got back, they'd probably close the roads, and we could be stuck at the ski lodge for days."

"Good deal!" Doug cried. "I'll turn around!"

"Just shut up and drive," Shannon said, shaking her head.

"Sorry," I said. "Guess it was a bad idea."

I wished we'd never *left* the lodge. I wished we'd never *gone* on this horrible ski weekend!

Suddenly the car sputtered and the tires slid again.

We all were silent until Doug pulled it back under control.

Then we went over a large bump. "Oh." For some reason I pictured a body under the car, some person lying stiff and frozen, half-buried under the snow and ice.

As I said, I'm real good at scaring myself.

"Just a bump," Doug said.

Everyone laughed, high-pitched, nervous laughter.

12

The road ran straight for a while, and then started to curve again. I made a clear circle on my fogged-up window to peer out. I could see a deep, tree-filled ravine that dropped straight down from the edge of the road.

If we started to slide, we'd plunge hood-first into the ravine!

The snow seemed to be blowing straight at the windshield, as if attacking us. A violent burst of wind shook the car.

"We're almost to the bottom of the mountain," Doug said, squinting through the windshield. "Maybe the snow won't be so bad once we reach the valley."

"Being home on Fear Street will be a *pleasure* after this," I said. "This is really scary!"

The road straightened out again when we reached the valley, but the snow was coming down just as hard as ever. We still hadn't seen another car either ahead of us or behind. Maybe the road was already closed and we didn't know it. There was no way to find out. Doug's car radio was broken too.

"I think I remember this area," Red said, energetically rubbing the steam off his window. "Listen, Doug, there's a county road coming up in a little bit. Turn left off this road and take it. It'll head in the same direction eventually."

"Huh? Take a little county road? Get real, Red." Doug pushed a little harder on the gas. The car barely responded.

"No, listen. The county guys get the snowplows out a lot faster than the state highway guys. You'll see. The county roads are always cleared way before the state roads."

Doug looked doubtful when he turned to see if Red was putting him on. But when we reached the intersection Red was talking about, and the small green sign proclaimed County Road 6, Doug made a left on to it, the tires whirring in protest. The car nearly spun in a complete circle. But Doug managed to straighten it out one more time, and we headed onto the county road.

"It's all woods and farms," I said glumly, staring out at the snow-covered pine trees. The world seemed to have gone black-and-white. The white of the snow was so bright, it was as if it blocked out all other colors.

"There's got to be a little town along this road, right?" Shannon asked hopefully. She pulled off her hood and scratched her copper-colored hair. She shifted again in her seat. "There's got to be a little town with a McDonald's, don't you think? Or one of those quaint little country restaurants? I'm so cold, I'm numb, Doug. I'm really numb."

"Maybe I'll stop the car and give you a massage," Doug said, giving her a devilish look.

"I'm serious!" Shannon protested.

I was still staring out the side window, freaking out on how all the color had disappeared from the world.

When I looked back up to the front, I saw the truck bearing down on us.

It was a huge, red moving van. Despite the blowing snow, I could see it through the windshield.

It suddenly felt as if everything were happening in slow motion.

The truck sounded its horn, a deep blast, the sound muffled by the snow.

It was coming right at us.

The road was narrow, too narrow for us to pass each other.

Doug slammed on the brakes, probably not the smartest thing to do. We started to slide—right into the path of the truck.

I closed my eyes.

I heard the truck's horn again, this time much louder. The sound was deafening. It made my bones vibrate.

I grabbed onto the back of Shannon's seat and prepared myself for the crash.

Then I felt the roar of the truck as it rolled past us.

It felt as if the car had been shoved away by the wind from the passing truck.

"All *right!*" Doug yelled happily.

"We made it!" I screamed, more surprised than anything else.

"We're gonna be okay from now on!" Doug declared, a big grin on his handsome face.

The car went a few more yards, sputtered, stalled, and then died.

chapter

3

No one moved or talked. And then we all began talking at once.

"There's plenty of gas," Doug said, staring down at the gauge. "So we'll get it going again."

"Give it a try," Red said, pushing his head between the seats to get a look at the dashboard dials. "If it doesn't kick over, I'll get out and take a look under the hood. Like I said, I'm real good with cars."

"Hey—back off, man. I know what I'm doing," Doug snapped, glaring angrily at Red.

Red slid back in his seat and raised his hands as if defending himself. "Just trying to help out, Boss."

"You can help out by shutting up!" Doug said.

"Doug—chill out," Shannon said, giving his shoulder a hard shove. "Don't take it out on Red."

Doug was hot-headed, but he was acting more uptight than usual. Who could blame him?

"I'm never getting home. Never!" Shannon cried.

I reached forward and patted her shoulder, trying to get her to calm down. To my surprise, she was trembling all over.

Doug turned the ignition key. There was a loud grinding noise. The engine coughed once, twice—and then turned over.

The roar of it starting up was one of the nicest sounds I'd ever heard. "Maybe we should stop and put on extra sweaters and stuff," I suggested, thinking we all might feel better if we were dressed more warmly.

"I don't want to stop again," Doug said, staring straight ahead, still sounding angry. "I'm afraid we might stall out again and you wimps might really freak."

"Look at the temperature gauge," Red said, his boyish face locked in a serious frown. "The engine is overheating. That's the problem."

"Thanks for the brilliant analysis, Mr. Goodwrench," Doug said sarcastically to Red.

"Overheating? How can *anything* overheat in this cold?!" Shannon cried.

"We're not going to get much farther," Red announced glumly, ignoring Doug's hostility.

"There's got to be a town," Shannon insisted, sounding really frightened. "They wouldn't build a road back here unless it went to a town—would they?"

The sky darkened. The snow continued to fall, gigantic flakes swirling in all directions, swept by the powerful winds. I could see nothing but tall pine trees now. Nothing but white-cloaked pines seeming to stretch forever.

The car hesitated again. Doug pushed hard on the gas.

"I guess I was wrong about this road," Red said, staring out through his window, his hands cupped over his eyes to cut down the glare. "It isn't any better than the state road."

"At least we're out of the mountains," I said, trying hard to look on the bright side.

"But we're nowhere!" Shannon protested. *"Nowhere!"*

"Wait a minute!" Red cried. His sudden excitement startled us all. "There's a house up there in the woods. I think we should stop."

"Huh? But we've got to get home," Doug said. He braked the car just the same, but kept the engine idling fast.

"We're not going to make it in this car," Red said matter-of-factly, his eyes still searching the woods. "We're going to stall out in the middle of nowhere. If we do, we really could freeze to death."

"I already have," Shannon said, reaching down to rub her ankles inside her boots.

"Red is right," I said. "It's going to be dark very soon. I really don't want to be stranded out here on this deserted road with no heater, no food, no nothing." I turned to Red. "Where's this house?"

"Up there." He pointed. The trees went up a low hill. From where I was sitting, I couldn't see anything but snow and tree trunks. I was surprised that Red could see a house so far from the road.

"It's up on that hill. Looks like a ski lodge or something. It's really big," he said. "Probably more than enough room to put us up for the night."

"And they'll have a phone," I said eagerly. "We can call our parents, let 'em know where we are."

"I'm doomed," Shannon said glumly. "My life is over."

"What makes you think whoever's up there will take us in?" Doug asked, more of a challenge to Red than a question.

"People are very hospitable in these parts," Red said. "I told you, I grew up around here. I just remember when I was a kid how friendly everyone was. Not like city people. No one would turn us away in a storm like this."

"I guess it's worth a try," I said reluctantly.

"Yeah. Let's go for it," Doug said, wiping the inside of the windshield with a balled-up tissue. "I could keep on driving. It's no sweat as far as I'm concerned. But I can see that you guys are whipped. Besides, this car has just about had it."

For some reason, I thought of Randy.

I hope you're enjoying your basketball game, safe and sound at home, I thought angrily.

I vowed to myself that I'd never go out with him again.

I hoped he was calling my house, wondering where I was, worrying about why I wasn't home yet.

Worrying along with my parents . . .

I looked at my watch. It was four-thirty. They wouldn't be worried yet. They wouldn't start to worry for another couple of hours. And by that time I would have called and told them about the storm.

"Just pull the car over to the side of the road," Red told Doug. "We'll leave all the ski stuff, just take your overnight bags and we'll walk up the hill to the house."

"I guess the car will be safe here," Doug said, turning off the engine.

"Whatever you do, don't lock it," Red warned, opening his door and climbing out into the snow. "The locks will freeze and you'll never be able to open the doors." He pulled on his blue wool ski cap and, staring up the hill, stretched his arms and legs.

I couldn't wait to do the same. Even though it had been less than two hours, I felt as if we'd been trapped in the car for months.

I climbed out and followed Red's gaze up the hill. Sure enough, there was a sprawling redwood house nestled among some pines. Smoke floated up from a stone chimney at the side. "Way to go, eagle eye!" I said, clapping Red on the back.

He turned and grinned at me. He was really attractive when he smiled like that. I turned back to see Doug helping Shannon out of the car. He put one arm around her waist and pushed her car door shut with the other hand.

"I would kill for a cup of coffee," Shannon said, shivering.

The snow clung to our hoods and hats and coats as we pulled our small overnight bags out of the trunk. The sky was really dark now. The wind seemed to grow colder even as we stood huddled at the back of the car.

"Wouldn't a nice hot bath feel good?" I said to Shannon.

"Oh yes!" Shannon exclaimed. "Come on—let's get up to that house!"

Doug slammed the trunk shut. We started walking, the four of us in a straight line, up the low, sloping hill along a wide path through the trees.

The snow was up to the tops of our boots, and in drifts it was even higher. It took a long time to get up the hill. But we were all so happy to be out of the car—with a warm house in view—that we didn't mind the snow, the cold, or the swirling winds.

We were just a few yards from the front porch when the feeling of dread came back to me. I had a sudden shiver—not from the cold—a shiver of fear.

But, of course, I ignored it.

It was too late to turn back.

Besides, it would be silly to give in to a momentary, irrational feeling of panic—right?

chapter

4

I was shivering by the time we made it up the sloping hill to the front porch, chilled through and through. The snow had gotten in over the tops of my boots, and my feet were wet and frozen.

Doug knocked loudly on the front door. Red stamped his boots up and down on the planks of the porch floor, knocking clumps of snow off. He smiled at me encouragingly. I guess I looked pretty pitiful.

Doug knocked again. Shannon, buried inside her big down ski jacket, had wrapped her arms tightly around herself for extra warmth, but she was shivering too.

The wind whipped around the side of the house, carrying wet snow with it. I reached up a gloved hand to feel my nose. It had no feeling. It was numb.

Frostbite City, I thought, unless someone opens that door now.

We heard footsteps inside the big house. They sounded louder, and finally the front door swung open.

"Whoooa!" The man seemed surprised to see us. He was tall and broad shouldered. He had scraggly brown hair that looked as if it hadn't been combed in days, and a short brown beard. He was wearing a red flannel shirt and baggy blue jeans that had been patched at one knee.

"Well, well—look what the cat dragged in!" he bellowed, eyeing us one at a time.

"Our car—" Doug started. "You see, the storm—" I think Doug was too cold to speak!

"Well, move it. Get your buns in here," the man said in a booming, deep voice. "Hurry—you're letting in the cold."

We rushed forward, bumping into one another in our eagerness to get inside. Once we were in, the man slammed the door and locked it.

I'd been staring at the bright snow for so long, it took awhile for my eyes to adjust to the room. There was no entranceway. Just one enormous front room with a cathedral ceiling and a big glass skylight at the top that provided a bit of light. There was a big stone fireplace against the far wall opposite a second-floor balcony, and in it several logs were burning, crackling loudly and sending up tall orange flames.

I'd never been so happy to see a fire in my life!

"Whooooeeee! You guys look frozen," the man said. "Get out of those wet boots, drop your coats over there"—he pointed to an alcove to our left—"and come warm your bods in front of the fire."

We obediently followed his instructions.

"Eva! Eva!" he shouted. "Get in here, gal. We've got unexpected company!"

"We were heading home, but we couldn't make it through the storm," Doug finally managed to explain, pulling off his boots, his gloves still on. "Our car didn't have a heater and—"

"Come on. Get your frozen buns over to the fire," the man interrupted, helping Shannon pull off her coat. "You're a pretty one," he told her. "I like redheads."

I saw Doug make a sour face. He never liked it when anyone came on to Shannon, even teasing.

"We don't mean to intrude," Red said, shaking the snow out of his hair.

"Hey—no problem," the man said. "Eva and me have plenty of room. This place used to be a ski lodge before they went and built the new highway. You kids are welcome to wait out the storm here."

"Thanks," Shannon said, hurrying over to the fire. "I don't think I could've stayed another minute in that freezing car."

"I'm Lou," the man said, kicking our boots up against the wall. "Lou Hitchcock. Where you kids from?"

"Shadyside," I said, examining my wool socks. They were soaked through. "Except for Red."

"I'm from Brockton," Red said, stopping at the

back of the long leather sofa that faced the fire. "I'm hitching a ride with these guys. I met them up at Pineview."

"The ski lodge?" Lou asked, scratching his beard with two stubby hands.

Before Red could answer, a young woman walked into the room, wiping her slender hands on a dishtowel. "Well, there's her nibs," Lou said, smiling. "This is my better half—Eva."

We all said hello at once. She looked younger than Lou, about twenty-five or so. She had very fine, curly blond hair that looked bleached, and she wore metal-rimmed glasses over blue eyes. She was wearing a red flannel shirt too. It looked like a tiny version of her husband's. And she wore straight-legged brown corduroy slacks and brown workboots.

"I certainly didn't expect visitors today," she said, sounding more than a little confused. She had a tiny voice. Seeing her next to Lou, I thought of a mouse next to a bear.

We introduced ourselves, repeating our names first for Eva and then for Lou, who insisted on vigorously shaking our still-frozen hands.

"These turkeys were driving in the snow. Got stranded," Lou said. "Guess they don't know the roads have all been closed. I told them this place ain't exactly a Holiday Inn, but we can make 'em comfortable till the snow stops."

Eva got a concerned look on her face, but didn't say anything. I had the feeling that she felt uncomfortable having four strange teenagers pop in from nowhere. I know I would! But all she said was, "I'll go put on some coffee. You kids look frozen."

I sat down on a white shag area rug, leaned my back against the leather sofa, and stretched my feet toward the fire. Man, did that feel good!

I looked up at Shannon, who was huddled beside Doug on one end of the long couch. She actually had a smile on her face, the first one I'd seen since we'd left the ski lodge.

"Man oh man, look at 'er snow!" Lou said, his voice booming off the high wooden rafters as he paced back and forth in front of us. "Listen to that wind. Some of the drifts are six feet deep! Unbelievable!" He stopped pacing in front of Shannon. "You're not bad, kid. Did I mention that I just love redheads?"

I couldn't tell whether Shannon was blushing or her face was just red from the cold, but she looked pretty uncomfortable. Lou was really staring at her!

I prayed that Doug would ignore it and keep his temper in check for once. These people were going to put us up for the night, after all.

It was taking awhile for my brain to unfreeze. I stared into the orange flames as if hypnotized. Everyone else in the room seemed to disappear for a bit. I guess I was exhausted just from the long, frightening drive.

Everything went out of focus, and I lost myself in the warm, flickering glow. When I came out of this comfortable daze, I suddenly remembered my parents. "Do you have a phone?" I asked Lou, who was sitting in a worn leather armchair at the far end of the couch, thumbing through a tattered magazine.

"Right! My parents!" Shannon cried, jumping up from the couch. "What am I going to tell them? I'm going to be grounded for life."

"Don't worry. We'll think of something," Doug reassured her, pulling her back down beside him.

Lou pointed to a low table underneath the balcony. "Phone's over there. You can give it a try. The lines were messed up this morning, but maybe it's okay now."

Doug, Shannon, and I scrambled toward the phone. Doug got to the table first, picked up the receiver, and listened. "There's static, but I think it's working," he said. He started to dial his parents.

I looked over toward the fire. Red had stretched out on the couch, his head on the padded arm. "Aren't you going to call home?" I asked.

"It can wait till later," he said. "They're not expecting me till the middle of the week, so they won't be worried." He raised his knees, reached forward, and pulled up his socks. One of them had a large hole at the toe.

"I can't hear too well!" Doug was shouting into the phone. He kept assuring his mom that he was okay. Shannon went next, and I could tell her parents were giving her a pretty bad time.

Eva came in with a big pot of coffee and a loaf of banana bread. I don't think coffee ever smelled so good. I hadn't realized it, but I was starving.

It was my turn to use the phone next. There was so

much static on the line, I could barely hear the dial tone. Finally I could hear the phone ringing at my house. It sounded a million miles away.

"You have reached the Munroes," my mother's voice came through the static. "I'm sorry, but no one is home right now . . ."

"I don't believe it!" I told Shannon. "I got the tape!"

Shannon shrugged. "Maybe it's not snowing this hard back in Shadyside."

I waited for the beep and left a message, trying to shout over the interference on the line. When I hung up, I realized I felt a little down. I'd really wanted to talk to them, to hear their voices.

They were usually home on Sunday evening. I had a creepy feeling that something bad had happened to them. I get this feeling a lot. I'm just a worrier, that's all. I can't help it.

I know it's childish. But there I was in a strange house somewhere, two hundred miles from home. I didn't even know where exactly. In the middle of the worst snowstorm I'd ever seen. And I just wanted to talk to my mom or dad and tell them what had happened.

I felt cheated, I guess. Abandoned in some small way.

The banana bread and coffee cheered me up a lot. I think we were all starving and hadn't realized it. We wolfed down the bread, and Eva came back with another one, which we also wolfed down.

"It was really nice of you to take us in, Lou," Red

said, still stretched out on the couch. Shannon and Doug were pressed close together on the other end of the couch. I had returned to my place on the rug in front of the fire.

"Don't mention it." Lou put down the magazine he'd been leafing through. I saw that it actually wasn't a magazine at all. It was a gun catalog.

"You guys like to hunt?" he asked, following my glance.

"Yeah, you bet," Doug said enthusiastically. "My dad takes me hunting all the time. I love it."

Lou laughed for some reason. His dark eyes seemed to light up. He pointed above the fireplace to two deer heads mounted on the stone chimney. I hadn't even noticed them till then. I guess I was too dazzled by the fire.

"See those beauties? I bagged both of those one morning last fall." He raised his arms into a pretend rifle, aimed up at the deer heads, and shouted, "Ka-plow ka-*plow!*"

"Ugh," said Shannon, making a face.

Lou laughed again. "Nothing like hunting," he said, staring at Shannon. "But I understand why you made that face, young lady. It's a real man's sport."

"Yeah. That's what my dad says too," Doug said, nodding his head in agreement. His black curly hair was matted down from the wool ski cap he'd worn all day, but it glowed in the firelight. "He lets me fire his hunting rifle when we go out. It has a pretty powerful kick, but I can handle it."

Of course you love hunting, Doug, I thought sarcastically. Doug was a pretty good guy. I mean, he was great looking with that dark hair and that really neat smile that made his eyes crinkle, and he had a good sense of humor and everything. But that macho side of him just turned me off completely.

Lou stared at Doug as if sizing him up. "So you can handle a gun, huh?"

Doug nodded, staring back at Lou as if accepting a challenge.

Please, please, Doug, I thought. Don't start up. Don't try to prove anything to Lou. Lou looks pretty macho himself.

I watched Lou walk over to a large, glass-encased gunrack on the wall in the corner. Doug and Red followed him. I glanced at Shannon, but she was staring up at the deer heads.

"Look at this beauty," Lou was saying, handing a large revolver to Doug, who took it and dutifully admired it. "And see this hunting rifle? Sheer perfection!" Lou exclaimed, an enthusiastic grin under his beard.

"Nice," Doug said. "That's a real beauty." He aimed it up at the deer heads and pretended to fire.

"Whoa. Careful. I keep 'em all loaded," Lou said, replacing the rifle in the rack and closing the glass cover. "Just in case."

Just in case *what?* I wondered.

"You can never be too careful with guns, though, I'll tell you," Lou said, leading the two boys back to the fire. "This ol' boy I knew, name of Harve. Harve

Dawkins. Harve liked to hunt in the snow. Crazy jackass. I'll bet he'd even go out on a day like this. Said it was more challenging."

"What did he hunt? Snowmen?" Red asked, then laughed his funny, high-pitched laugh.

"No. Deer," Lou replied seriously. "Harve always said he could see the deer better in the snow. They couldn't hide as well. That's what he said. But ol' Harve made one little mistake, you see. I mean, it may be easy to spot the deer in the snow, but it's a heckuva lot harder to spot a hunter. Know what I'm saying?"

Doug nodded and chuckled loudly. Red was starting to look very uncomfortable. Shannon just stared grim faced into the fire. I think she was enjoying the story as little as I was.

"Well, I imagine you guessed the ending already," Lou said, sort of bobbing up and down on the heels and toes of his work boots as he talked. "That's right. Poor Harve got his head blown off by some fool hunter!"

Lou threw his head back and laughed.

Doug joined in, shaking his head as he laughed. Red looked back at me and rolled his eyes, as if to say, What's with these characters?

I didn't see the funny part. "This Harve was a friend of yours?" I asked.

"Yeah," Lou replied. And for some reason, that made him laugh even harder. "Can you believe it?" he asked, shaking his head. "I mean, can you believe that crazy jackass?"

What a hideous story, I thought, staring at Lou's gunrack behind him and suddenly feeling another chill.

Red was still peering at me. I think he was reading my thoughts. Doug was just shaking his head, a wide grin on his face. He headed back to Shannon on the couch.

"Maybe we'll all go out hunting later, what do you say?" Lou asked, looking at Red.

"Nothing doing," Red said quickly. "I'm staying right here by the fire. You couldn't get me to go walking in that snow for anything!"

Lou made a face. Red's answer didn't seem to please him.

I suddenly felt chilled again, despite the fire. Chilled and very uncomfortable. Maybe it was just the long day. Maybe it was the guns and Lou's story, the way he thought it was so hilarious that a friend had been killed.

I got up and walked over to the large window that almost covered an entire wall. The wind howled in the dark night without letup, blowing waves of snow against the glass.

Don't let yourself get worked up about Lou, I told myself. He's okay. He was nice enough to take us all in, after all.

I scolded myself for being a snob. You're just not used to people like him, Ariel, I told myself. So he makes you uncomfortable. Well, he was just trying to be friendly. He's obviously uncomfortable with us too. That's all.

I turned away from the window and walked into the kitchen. It was big and warm and smelled of apples and cinnamon. It looked like a ski-lodge kitchen with dark wood paneling and exposed rafters overhead. A large, old-fashioned range stood against one wall. Something was boiling in a round copper pot on the stovetop. Beyond that, I saw a cozy breakfast nook with a long wooden table, wooden cabinets on three walls, and a large, curtained window that looked out on the back.

Eva was at the double sink, washing the coffee cups we had used. "Hi," I said uncertainly. My voice startled her. I guess she'd been thinking about something.

She looked at me over the rims of her glasses. "I'm sorry. I've forgotten your name," she said, reddening slightly.

"Ariel," I said. "I'm sorry to bother you, Eva, but I'm still cold. Do you think I could have a cup of tea? I'll be glad to make it myself."

"No trouble," she said, drying her hands. "Now let's see . . ." She walked past me and reached up to open one of the cabinets. She stood on tiptoes and started to sort through the contents of each shelf, looking for the tea.

"Can I help?" I asked.

"No. I'll find it," she said. She closed the cabinet door and opened another.

It suddenly struck me that this was extremely odd.

I mean, if this was Eva's kitchen, why didn't she have any idea where the tea was?

33

Was I reading too much into this?

Or was it definitely weird?

"That Lou—he never puts anything back in the same place twice," Eva said suddenly as if reading my mind. "Okay! Here it is." She reached up to the top shelf and pulled down a packet of tea bags. "Is Earl Grey okay?"

"Yes, fine," I said. I gave her a warm smile, but she avoided meeting my eyes and quickly walked over to the island counter in the middle of the kitchen. She's very shy, I realized.

I took a seat on one of the benches at the kitchen table and watched her put on the tea kettle. "This is a great house," I said, struggling to make conversation.

She didn't turn around, just gave a vague shrug. "It's so big and drafty," she said, her voice barely reaching me.

At that point Doug came in. I was glad to see him. I wasn't having much luck making conversation with Eva. "What's happening?" he asked. "I wondered where you went."

"Well, you found me," I said, smiling. "Just having some tea."

"I have to run upstairs for a bit," Eva interrupted, tucking a flap of her flannel shirt into the front of her jeans. "Just pour the water when the kettle boils."

"Thanks," I said, looking at Doug. Eva left the room silently.

"She's so quiet," Doug observed. "She and Lou are a weird couple, don't you think?"

"I guess," I said.

I started to say something else—but stopped. Doug and I both cried out in surprise when we heard the snap of a gunshot right behind us!

chapter
5

"What was that?" I cried, my heart pounding.

For a brief second Doug appeared as frightened as I was. But then he quickly recovered. Good old Mr. Macho. "It sounded like—"

He was staring down at the floor behind the kitchen table. I turned around and followed his eyes.

"Oh my!"

It wasn't a gunshot we'd heard. It was the snap of a mousetrap on the floor.

A tiny brown mouse was struggling in the trap—the metal bar clamped over its neck. Its little black eyes bulged wide, and its tiny legs thrashed violently, scratching against the flat, wooden part of the trap.

And then all at once they stopped.

I turned away. "How horrible," I said.

Doug laughed.

"No. I mean it. It would be so horrible to step into a trap like that, to know that you walked right into your own death."

"Yeah. A real bummer," Doug said, making fun of me.

He walked over to the corner, bent down, and picked up the trap with the dead mouse pinned inside. "Like a snack with your tea?"

"Ugh. You're really gross," I said, moving my head away. "You really are an insensitive clod!"

That made him grin even more. He walked over to the double sink, opened the cabinet door beneath it, and tossed the dead mouse in a trash can. "Well, maybe I'm not as sensitive as you, Ariel. Nobody is."

I'd known Doug since third grade, long before I'd known Shannon. We'd gotten used to talking to each other this way, sort of like brother and sister.

"I had no choice. I had to be sensitive," I said. "I mean, my parents named me after Shakespeare."

"Your name is Shakespeare?"

This was a running gag with us. We'd gone through this routine a million times, but we both still thought it was a riot.

The kettle started to whistle. I tossed my hair behind my shoulders and walked over to the big stove to make my tea. "I'm Ariel the sprite," I said. "Watch how you talk to a sprite."

"I could go for a Sprite right now. I'm dying of thirst," Doug said. He laughed and slapped the counter.

I wondered if we'd ever grow tired of that awful joke

as I carried the kettle over to the cup and poured the steaming water. Then I dropped the tea bag in. Peering out into the darkness beyond the kitchen window, I could see that it was still snowing hard. The sky was black behind the snow-covered trees. The wind continued to howl and blow.

"I don't know what you're so cheerful about," I said, suddenly feeling very worried. "We're never getting out of here."

"They'll have the road cleared by morning," he said. "No problem." I could tell he wasn't as confident as he was trying to sound. Sometimes I wished he would just drop the tough-guy pose and let himself be real. But then I thought there was no point in *both* of us sitting around biting our fingernails down to the quick.

"Hey—what's with you and Red?" he asked, deliberately changing the subject then. He plopped down across from me at the table.

I took a sip of the tea and burned my tongue. "What do you mean? Nothing."

"I've seen him looking at you," Doug said, obviously teasing me. "You know, checking you out."

"Give me a break," I said. "Red's a nice guy. I kinda like him, I guess."

"The guy saved our lives by finding this place," Doug said, becoming serious.

I started to agree, but we were interrupted by another loud noise. This one was definitely not a gunshot or the snap of a mousetrap. It came from the living room, and it sounded like the roof was crashing down!

Doug and I jumped up from the table and tore into the large main room. Lou was standing in the middle of the room, a beer can in one hand, looking concerned. Red and Shannon were standing by the fireplace, the orange firelight causing their frightened faces to flicker and glow.

"What was that, Lou?" Eva called down from upstairs.

"Sounded like it was out front," Lou called up to her.

He dropped his beer can onto a side table and walked to the front door, taking long, unsteady strides, probably the effect of having had several beers.

The four of us were right behind him as he pulled on the big front door. A blast of frozen air rushed into the room as if it had been waiting for the door to open.

Lou staggered back, holding on to the doorknob. Then he leaned forward, peering out onto the porch. "It's a tree limb," he said, and started cursing at the top of his lungs. He turned back to us. His hair and beard were dotted with large, white snowflakes. "A tree limb," he repeated. "Probably couldn't take the weight of the snow."

"Please—close the door," Shannon said, shivering.

Lou poked his head back out. Another gust of frozen wind invaded the room, bringing a spray of snow with it.

"It went through the porch roof," Lou called in to us. "Lucky it didn't land right on the house." He came back in and pushed the door closed. He shook his head to get the snow off.

"Let's go pull it out of there," suggested Doug. "I could use a little exercise." He started across the room toward the coat alcove.

"Yeah. Thanks," Lou said, raising his eyebrows questioningly at Red. "You coming too?"

"Yeah. I'll help," Red said, sounding a lot less eager than Doug, who already had his ski jacket on and was heading out the front door.

Lou pulled a down coat off a peg near the door and put it on, fumbling with the zipper.

That's strange, I thought. The sleeves of that coat are way too short for him.

The three guys disappeared out the front door. Shannon and I went into the kitchen to get away from the cold air. I poured her a cup of tea, and we took our cups and sat in front of the fire. From out front we could hear the voices of Doug, Red, and Lou as they struggled to remove the tree branch from the porch.

"I guess we needed a little more excitement today," Shannon said, staring into the fire.

"It's been quite a day," I agreed. I thought of Randy for some reason. I wondered what he was doing right then, whether he was worried about me.

What's to be worried about? I asked myself.

You're safe and warm.

So why didn't I feel safe?

And why couldn't I warm up even though I was sitting directly in front of a fire drinking hot tea?

"Red's really nice," Shannon said, giving me a meaningful look.

I shrugged. "Yeah. He's a good guy."

We heard a crash outside. The guys must have managed to pull the limb off the porch roof.

"Do you think Lou is, you know—all right?" Shannon asked. I could see that she was nervous, so I tried to be cheerful and up.

"It was nice of him to take us in like this," I said. But my eyes went up to the gunrack in the corner, and I found myself thinking about that awful story Lou had told and how funny he thought it was.

A few minutes later the front door burst open. Doug, Red, and Lou came tromping into the room, their faces red from the cold.

"I told you to let me pull!" Lou yelled angrily at Doug. "You got a hearing problem or something?"

"Next time you can pull out your own tree limb," Doug said. He stared back at Lou, challenging him, standing up to him.

"Everything okay?" Eva called from upstairs. I wondered why she hadn't come down and joined us by the fire.

"Yeah. I guess. Big Shot here has a little problem following directions." He glared at Doug, who twisted his head away. "But we got the thing cleared away!" Lou shouted up to her. He stamped his work boots to get the snow off. Then he unzipped the ill-fitting down

41

jacket, fussing with some ski-lift tickets that were hanging from the zipper, and tossed the jacket back up onto its peg.

"Lou and Doug are a bad combination," I whispered to Shannon.

Her eyes on Doug, she nodded in agreement. "Especially if Lou keeps staring at me like a hungry puppy," she whispered back. "You know how jealous Doug can be."

"Lou's been drinking," I whispered. "A lot, I think. That isn't helping matters."

"We've got to get Doug to cool out," Shannon whispered. "Or else we could be out in the snow by dinner time." She walked over and took Doug's arm to calm him.

A short while later Lou and Doug had seemingly made their peace. All of us except Eva were seated around the fire, eating chili and listening to Lou recount how he had been in a much worse storm than this once, trapped in a cabin with three beautiful women. As he told this story, he stared at Shannon the whole time.

Lou disappeared into the kitchen, then returned carrying another can of beer. "Hey, you monkeys are so lucky," he said, standing in front of the fireplace, his red flannel shirt untucked in front, his brown hair still damp from the snow and matted down on his forehead.

"Being caught in a storm like this isn't exactly lucky," Shannon said from one end of the couch.

"Yeah. But you got in a great weekend of skiing

first—right?" Lou said, turning around to stir the fire with a wrought-iron poker. "I used to love skiing. Way before I met Eva. But I haven't gone in years."

That's strange, I thought. There were lift tickets on the zipper of the jacket Lou had just been wearing. Well, that proves it, I thought. That jacket definitely isn't his.

But so what?

What did *that* prove?

Why was I being so suspicious of everything? Just my nature, I guessed.

Maybe part of my problem was that I was exhausted. I hadn't realized it. But I suddenly crashed—I suddenly felt too tired to move.

Lou was now talking about some ski trip he had taken years before. His voice drifted in and out of my consciousness. "And that crazy fool broke his leg in less than thirty seconds," I heard him say. Another one of his supposedly hilarious stories.

I took a final spoonful of chili, excused myself, and carried the bowl into the kitchen, where Eva was busily putting dishes and silverware into the dishwasher.

She had the most unhappy expression on her face. For a moment I thought she was close to tears. But her face went blank when she saw me, and she turned her back to me.

I asked if she'd show me where to sleep, and then I followed her up the creaking wooden stairs to the balcony landing. It was much warmer upstairs. As she led me down the narrow hallway, I peered over the balcony railing at my friends below. Shannon had snuggled up against Doug on the couch. Red was poking the fire now. Lou continued to talk, gesturing with the beer can in his hand, his booming voice echoing off the wooden rafters just above my head, his eyes trained on Shannon.

"I think we put your bag in this room," Eva said, pushing open a door and flicking on the light.

I followed her into a small guest bedroom, white painted walls, a curtained window that overlooked the front porch, a double bed, a dresser, and a straight-back wooden chair beside it.

"Watch your head," Eva warned, pointing to the steep slant of the ceiling.

"That quilt sure looks cozy," I said, cheered by the sight of the heavy maroon quilt on the bed. I couldn't wait to get undressed and get under it.

"If you need anything, just yell," she said. She disappeared before I could thank her.

It didn't take me long to tear off my clothes, pull on a nightgown from my bag, turn out the light, and slide under the covers. The bed was soft and not too cold. The springs squeaked with every move I made. But I was so exhausted, I didn't care.

At last I felt safe and secure under the big, heavy quilt.

I must have fallen asleep the minute my head hit the overstuffed feather pillow. I slept a dreamless sleep for I-don't-know-how-long. I don't think I moved.

I was awakened by the sound of the front door closing.

I sat up, wide awake. And listened.

Someone had either gone out—or come in.

My heart pounding, I climbed out from under the quilt and walked to the window. I pressed my forehead against the cold glass and stared across the porch roof to the sloping front lawn.

No one there.

The snow was still falling, smaller flakes now. It seemed to sparkle, almost too bright to be real. For a moment I had the feeling that this *wasn't* real, that it was all just a dream that I'd soon awaken from and find myself—where?

I heard floorboards creak downstairs.

Someone had come in and was walking around down there.

I tiptoed to the bedroom door, pulled it open, and crept silently along the hall to the balcony landing.

The fire in the fireplace had nearly burned out. Dark red embers popped and sizzled among black shadows that had once been logs.

Another loud creaking floorboard. A cough.

There were no lights on.

Whoever it was had chosen to walk around in the dark.

I started to call out, but lost my nerve.

Who would come into the house in the middle of the night? Especially on a night like this?

Who would creep around without turning on a light?

I jumped at the sound of something crashing to the floor down there.

Was someone trying to wreck the place? Had someone broken in?

If all the lights were out, the house would look deserted from the outside. Was it some squatter down there, someone who had decided to break in and spend the night out of the storm?

Horrifying thoughts flashed through my mind, pictures of masked men carrying bloody hatchets and chainsaws.

I shivered. It was cold out there on the balcony. I decided to get back under my warm, safe quilt.

I turned around and started back to my room.

I reached the doorway and froze. My breath caught in my throat.

Footsteps. Coming closer.

Someone was climbing up the back stairs.

chapter
6

My first impulse was to dart into my room, close the door, and hide under the quilt.

But my curiosity was even stronger than my fear.

The footsteps drew closer. The wooden stairs creaked loudly.

I stood frozen in my doorway, my heart pounding, peering into the darkness, ready to duck back into my room if the intruder was someone dangerous.

A dark figure appeared at the head of the stairs.

I realized then that I'd been holding my breath. I let it out silently, still staring into the darkness.

Once on the landing, the figure moved quickly.

He strode right up to me.

I thought of trying to get away, but I had waited too long. It was too late.

He stopped in front of me, leaning toward me in the darkness.

"Red!" I whispered.

He raised a finger to his lips. "Ssshhh." He put his hands on my shoulders and guided me back into my room, closing the door silently behind us.

"Red—your hands are frozen! What do you want?"

Again he motioned for me to talk softly. I fumbled around until I found the lampswitch and clicked on the light. Red was in his coat. His ears were bright red from the cold.

"How come you're awake?" he whispered. He unzipped his jacket and tugged it off.

I was cold, so I climbed under the quilt. "You woke me up," I told him, whispering. "I heard the front door close. Where did you go? It must be after midnight."

He sat down on the edge of the bed and rubbed his hands together to warm them. "I couldn't sleep," he said. He brushed back his wavy red hair with one hand. He looked like a little boy when he did that. I realized I was very attracted to him.

"My room's down the hall, next to Lou and Eva's," he said, staring nervously at the closed door. "I could hear them through the wall. They were shouting at each other, arguing about something."

"Well, they're married," I said, pulling the quilt up to my chin. "Married people argue all the time."

"No. Not like this," Red insisted, leaning toward me and whispering excitedly. "It wasn't just an argument. It was a real fight. I'm pretty sure Lou hit her."

"Are you sure?"

"Yeah. I heard the sound of it. Then I heard her cry

out. Just a short cry. And then he shouted something and it got very quiet."

"Quiet? What do you mean?" I asked, cold again despite the quilt.

"I mean, quiet. I couldn't hear them anymore. Not a sound. It—it was scary, Ariel."

"That's awful. Do you think she's all right? Lou gives me the creeps. We've just got to get out of here! What were they fighting about?" The words tumbled out of me. I was starting to feel panicky.

"I don't know. I couldn't hear." He stood up and began to pace back and forth beside the bed. "I mean, I tried not to hear. I just wanted to get to sleep, you know. But then when he hit her and it got so quiet, I got scared."

"What should we do? Should we call the police, do you think?" My head was spinning. I couldn't think clearly.

"I don't know. I don't think so," Red said thoughtfully. "Maybe they just went to sleep. Maybe he didn't hit her. But it sure sounded like it. I just sat there, listening. The silence was worse than the fighting. I couldn't stand just sitting there, so I went downstairs and took a walk in the snow."

"Isn't it freezing cold out there?" I asked.

"It's not that bad," he said, looking down at me. "It was kind of beautiful, actually. The snow is so white, so clean. It doesn't look real. The wind has died down, so it's real quiet. I just had to get out of the house. I—I think Lou is a little nuts."

"He had an awful lot to drink," I said.

"I thought he and Doug were going to get into a fight. All night Lou kept teasing Doug, giving him a hard time. I think Lou was trying to provoke him. I can't wait to get out of here," Red said. He sat back down on the edge of the bed.

"At least we're not trapped in the car somewhere," I said. And then I added, "Thanks to you."

That seemed to please him. He smiled at me. He had a great smile, the kind of smile that made his eyes crinkle.

He leaned forward and brought his face close to mine.

He started to kiss me.

I started to kiss him back.

He pressed harder and started to wrap his arms around me.

I pulled my face away. "No, Red. I don't think we should," I said, my heart pounding.

He seemed to be hurt, but it lasted only a second.

He sat back up and shook his head as if to shrug it off. "Sorry," he said.

"No need to apologize," I said, suddenly feeling like a jerk. "I just don't think we should—"

"You're right," he said quickly and blushed.

He looked so cute, I wanted to grab him and kiss him again. I was glad he was being so nice.

"See you in the morning," he said. "I'm sure they'll get the roads cleared by then."

He disappeared down the hallway, shutting the door behind him. I sat up for a while, thinking about him. I could still taste his lips on mine. He's a really nice guy, I decided.

Nicer than Randy.

I closed my eyes and sank down into the pillow.

When I opened them, it was morning.

I woke up confused. It took me a while to remember where I was. I could smell bacon frying downstairs and realized that I was really hungry.

I pulled myself out of the warm bed, hurried to the frost-covered window, and peered out. The bright sunshine forced me to squint. It had stopped snowing during the night, but gusts of wind were tossing swirls of snow into the air. Deep drifts leaned against tree trunks, forming smooth, sparkling white hills.

I looked beyond the front yard to the road. But all I could see was an unending sea of white. No sign of any road crew.

Hearing voices in the hall, I searched through my bag and then pulled on my last clean clothes, a pair of green corduroy slacks, a T-shirt, and my heaviest sweater. I brushed the tangles out of my hair, then tied it behind my head in a ponytail. Then I hurried down to breakfast. The smell of bacon was driving me crazy!

"Hey—here's Blondie. Good morning, Bright Eyes!" Lou called cheerily.

He was at the stove, tending a big frying pan of scrambled eggs. He was wearing the same red flannel shirt as the day before, not tucked in, and baggy, black trousers. Shannon, Doug, and Red were already seated around the long kitchen table, quietly drinking coffee. The sunlight coming through the big kitchen window was almost blindingly bright.

"The snow stopped!" Shannon announced happily as if I wouldn't have already noticed.

"The plows should be through anytime now," Lou said, bringing the pan of eggs to the table and ladling out big portions for everyone. "Help yourself to orange juice, Blondie," he told me, motioning toward the carton on the table.

I thanked him and poured myself a big glass.

"The radio says there's another storm on the way," Doug said with a mouthful of eggs. "So we should get going as soon as we can."

"You turkeys better wait for the plows," Lou warned. "You don't have chains on your car, do you?"

"No," Doug said, reaching across the table for a second helping of bacon.

"Of course not. You wouldn't want to do anything practical, would you? Well, take it from me, Bozos, without chains you'll never make it. I was out earlier this morning. Some of the drifts are as tall as me!"

"Wow," I said to be polite. That was about the best I could do. My brain still wasn't awake.

I suddenly realized that Eva wasn't downstairs. "Where's Eva?" I asked.

Lou carried the empty frying pan to the sink and ran hot water into it. "I'm giving my better half a treat," he said, without turning around. "I'm letting her sleep in."

Red looked at me and I looked at him.

My stomach turned over, remembering what Red had heard during the night.

I dug into my eggs, but my appetite was gone. I wondered if Eva was okay up there.

Thank God, I thought, we'll be out of this place in an hour or so, and we'll never have to see these people again.

That thought cheered me up a lot. Everyone seemed to be in a good mood, knowing that we'd soon be on our way home to Shadyside.

After breakfast Doug headed to the front room to get his coat. "Where you going, Big Fella?" Lou asked, following him.

"I thought I'd go out and check on the car," Doug said.

"Waste of time," Lou told him. "You might as well wait till the road crew comes through."

"Well, I just want to see if the old wreck will start," Doug said, pulling on his boots. "The battery is pretty weak. I might need a jump start."

"I'll go with you," I volunteered. I really felt like some fresh air. "I haven't been in snow this deep since I was a kid."

"Hey, I'll go too," Red said, grabbing his coat.

"Count me out," Shannon said. "Since Eva isn't down yet, I'll help out with the dishes, Lou."

Lou smiled at her gratefully. He followed her back into the kitchen, scratching his beard with both hands. He stopped in the doorway to the kitchen and turned around. "I still don't know what your hurry is," he said to Doug, shaking his head. "You are the *stubbornest* jackass. Glad I'm not your father."

"Me too," Doug muttered. "I just want to start the thing up. We won't try to leave till the road is cleared."

I suddenly found myself wondering why Lou didn't want Doug to go check on the car. Why did he keep discouraging us from leaving? It almost seemed as if Lou was trying to keep us there.

But that was a crazy idea.

I wrapped my blue wool scarf around me, pulled my ski cap down over my ears, and followed Red and Doug out the front door.

The snow didn't make a sound as we made our way down the sloping front yard. It was like walking in cake batter, very cold cake batter. That's how wet and heavy it was.

"It's over the top of my boots!" I cried.

"This is great!" Doug said. He bent down, scooped up a big handful of snow, and quickly made a snowball. He tossed it playfully at me, but I ducked, and it sailed over my head, breaking up and landing silently back on the snow.

"Let's try jogging," Red suggested and tried to run, raising his skinny legs high, slipping and sliding with each step—until he fell face forward into a deep drift.

"Bad idea," I said, laughing as I helped to pull him up. But he pulled the other way, catching me off-guard, and I fell on top of him. I rolled off quickly. We were both laughing. We kept rolling. It felt so great!

"Hey—stop goofing around," Doug said, sounding annoyed.

"What's your problem?" I asked, getting up and brushing the snow that clung to the front of my jacket.

"This is serious," Doug said, picking up his pace. "You want to get out of here, don't you?"

"No. I want to stay all day and roll in the snow," I said sarcastically. "The snow is so deep, it's hard to resist rolling in it," I continued. Red agreed, laughing.

"Well, resist it," Doug said.

We had reached the road. At least, we thought we had. The drifts were so deep, it was hard to tell where the front yard ended and the road began.

"We parked it across the road just around that turn," Doug said, holding a hand up to his forehead to shield his eyes from the bright, white glare.

Red and I followed him around the turn in the road, slapping at our pants to get the snow off.

Suddenly Doug stopped.

His mouth had dropped open in surprise, and he looked very bewildered.

I followed his gaze. The road curved once and then straightened out. The snowdrifts followed the curve of the road.

"Oh no!" I cried, realizing what Doug had seen right away.

The car was gone.

chapter

7

The three of us stood staring down the empty road. It was almost like staring at that blank piece of white paper my dad used to show me.

A gust of wind shook snow from the trees. But I couldn't appreciate the beauty of it.

At that moment I felt only dread.

Doug and Red went running around the curve of the road, and I followed. The road straightened out to reveal a deep ravine on the far side.

"We parked it right by that tree," Doug said, pointing, his breath coming out in puffs of white.

His boots crunching into the high snow, Red ran up to the edge of the ravine. He looked down, leaning over the deep drop.

It's so deserted here, I thought. Who could have come and stolen Doug's car? Especially in such an incredible snowstorm.

"There it is!" Red yelled, pointing down into the gorge.

Doug and I rushed up to the edge and stared down, following the direction of his finger.

Sure enough, the car was on its side, half-buried in snow at the bottom of the chasm.

"I don't believe it!" Doug said, balling his gloved hands into tight fists at his side. "I parked away from the edge. I *know* I did."

"Maybe the plows came through during the night and pushed it over," Red suggested, wiping blowing snow from his cheeks with the back of his glove.

Doug and I both turned around to look at the road. "No one has plowed here," I said gloomily. "The snow is totally smooth."

"Maybe the wind blew it over the edge," Red said thoughtfully.

Or maybe Lou pushed it over, I thought.

I knew it was dumb. But you can't control what pops into your mind.

Back at the house Lou had been trying to discourage us from leaving early. And then he even tried to discourage us from going out and taking a look at the car.

Why?

Because he had pushed the car down into the ravine?

Because he wanted to keep us here for some reason?

Stop it. Stop it. Stop it.

I knew I had to force those thoughts from my mind. But I kept thinking—we're trapped. We're trapped in

57

the middle of nowhere. With strangers. With strangers with guns.

"Now what? We're trapped here," Doug said, his words echoing my thoughts. For once he wasn't putting on a macho act. He looked genuinely upset.

"No, wait—Lou can get us to town," I said, pulling him away from the edge of the chasm. "I'm sure we can rent a car or take a bus or something from there."

"The car doesn't look too damaged," Red said, still staring down at it, his cheeks bright red from the cold. "We can call a tow truck. They can probably pull it out. You never know. It might start right up."

Doug looked doubtful. I pulled him by the arm. "Come on. Let's go back to the house and call. We're not getting anywhere standing here and feeling sorry for ourselves."

We had left the house in such good spirits, believing that we'd soon be on our way home. But now we trudged back up to the house in unhappy silence.

I kept my head down, trying to avoid the blinding glare of the sunlight. I thought about my cozy room at home. I wondered what my mom and dad were doing right then.

I'll be home by tonight, I told myself.

But I wasn't sure I believed it.

Lou greeted us cheerily at the front door. "Hey, my little snow bunnies. Look—I caught us some lunch!" he said, and held up a mousetrap with a freshly killed mouse in it. The trap had snapped the poor little mouse across the middle, and some of its insides were oozing out.

A wide grin spread across Lou's face. "Just about snapped the little sucker in two."

"Lou—give us a break," Red said, pulling off his cap.

"That's really gross," I said, my eyes still adjusting to the room after the brightness of the snow.

"Hey—what's your problem?" Lou asked, lowering the mousetrap from view.

"Our problem is, our car went over the side of that gulley," Doug said glumly. He looked down, saw that he was dripping water on the alcove carpet, and leaned against the wall to pull off his boots.

"All the way to the bottom?" Lou asked, disappearing into the other room, I hoped in order to throw away the mouse.

"Well, just about. It's on its side," Doug called.

Shannon appeared suddenly on the balcony just above us. She was brushing her coppery hair. "What's going on, guys? We ready to go?"

"Not exactly," I called up to her, a heavy feeling in the pit of my stomach. "The car's wrecked. I mean, it fell into a gorge."

"How?" Shannon cried.

Before anyone could reply, Lou reappeared, wiping his hands on a dishtowel. "You sure you passed your parking test?" he asked Doug, grinning.

"Hey—" Doug didn't appreciate the joke. I knew he wanted to punch Lou, but somehow he managed to control himself.

"Maybe it can be pulled out. There's a tow service in town," Lou said. He tossed the towel onto the couch, walked over to the phone on the little table in the corner, and began to flip through the Yellow Pages.

"They're probably pretty busy today. I imagine you're not the only bozos who got stuck in this storm." He found the number. "But what the heck. Might as well give them a call."

He picked up the phone receiver and held it up to his ear.

The smile faded from his face. "Hey—"

He tapped the buttons on the phone.

"Hey—"

He turned to us and frowned.

"What's the matter, Lou?" I asked, knowing the answer before he even said it.

"Phone's dead. I guess the lines are down."

chapter

8

Lou swore and slammed the receiver down. "I don't believe this!" he bellowed. "The phone's perfectly okay during the storm. Then it goes out when the storm's over! Does that make any sense?"

He angrily picked up the telephone and heaved it against the wall.

"Take it easy, Lou," Red said, looking scared.

"Probably ice on the phone wires," Doug said quietly. I think he was enjoying seeing Lou so upset.

We all stared at Lou as he furiously paced back and forth, swearing about the phone. I realized that my suspicions had been all wrong.

It was obvious that Lou hadn't pushed Doug's car into the ravine. If Lou had wanted to keep us there for some reason, he wouldn't be carrying on like a lunatic about the phone lines being down.

That thought didn't make me feel any better. I still had that heavy feeling in the pit of my stomach. I still felt trapped.

No car. No phone.

No way home.

I guess Shannon saw how unhappy I was. After she came downstairs, she sat down next to me on the couch, giving me a reassuring smile and a pat.

This is a switch, I thought. Shannon trying to cheer *me* up.

"What's going to go out next—the lights?" Lou was screaming at no one in particular. "One little snowstorm and everything falls to pieces!" He started scratching his beard furiously as he let out a string of curses.

"There's got to be some way to get to the nearest town," I said quietly, trying to get him to stop ranting and raving.

"Well, if those lazy idiots on the road crew ever get off their butts and plow, we can take the Jeep to town!" Lou exclaimed.

Doug's mouth dropped open. "You have a Jeep?"

"Yeah. In the barn," Lou said.

"Well, it has four-wheel drive, right? Won't it get us to town?" Doug asked.

"Hey, he's right," Red quickly agreed.

Lou shook his head. He picked up the receiver, listened, then slammed it down again. "No way," he said, kicking at the side of the leather armchair. "The snow is too deep. I don't care if we had *eight*-wheel drive. We wouldn't make it. Not with the drifts up to our necks."

"I bet we could make it," Doug insisted excitedly. "Jeeps are made for roads like this."

Lou glared at Doug. "Mister Expert," he muttered under his breath.

"It's worth a try, don't you think, Lou?" Red asked eagerly.

Lou raked a hand back through his greasy, matted-down hair. "I don't know. . . ."

"Let's just try!" I said. "We've *got* to get to a phone and call our parents to let them know what's happened."

"Yeah. They'll be frantic," Shannon added.

"Well, I wouldn't want your mommies to be frantic," Lou said in a babyish little voice. "I guess maybe we should give the Jeep a try. The radio said another storm is heading our way. It would be good to get you turkeys home before it hits. And before you eat me outta house and home."

"Okay!" I cried enthusiastically, jumping to my feet. "Let's go!"

"Hold your horses," Lou said, frowning. "I've got a few things to do first. Why don't you guys get all packed up and then go outside and throw snowballs or something. I'll be out as soon as I can."

"Sounds good," I said. I was so happy we'd soon be getting out of there.

"Just remember—don't eat the yellow snow!" Lou said and laughed as if he'd said something really hilarious.

"Is there a rent-a-car place in town?" Shannon asked.

"Yeah. I think so," Lou said. "Sure. There must be." He tried the telephone once more. Then, cursing under his breath, headed for the kitchen.

The four of us hurried upstairs to get our bags. It took two minutes to pack. I think everyone was as eager as I was to get out of this house.

We cheerfully carried our bags down and left them by the kitchen door. Then we pulled on our coats and boots and went outside to enjoy the snow while we waited for Lou. A few gray clouds were slowly drifting our way from the north, but most of the sky was still bright blue, and the gentle waves of snow that covered the backyard were sparkling and beautiful.

Behind the house was the barn, an old wooden structure, which looked as if it hadn't been painted in a hundred years. Snow clung to the slanted roof in deep drifts, making it look like a barn in an antique postcard.

Beyond the barn stretched what had to be a frozen lake. It was covered with snow that sparkled in the late-morning sun.

"Too bad we don't have ice skates! We could sweep off the snow and skate on the lake!" I cried, a bit overwhelmed by the unbelievable beauty of the scene.

"Maybe they have some in the barn," Doug suggested, stepping quickly across the snow, his boots disappearing in the deep drifts.

"We don't have time for skating," Shannon called to him. "We're getting out of here, remember?"

"YAAY!" I cried happily, clapping my gloves together.

"Duck!" Red cried.

I didn't understand him in time. A snowball hit me hard on the shoulder. I looked up to see Doug laughing.

"Good packing snow!" he shouted.

"Let's see about that!" I said, scooping up a handful. It *was* good packing snow. Nice and wet. I heaved a snowball at Doug. Not hard enough. It plopped into the snow at his feet.

Shannon had better aim. She caught him right in the chest. It made a very satisfying plopping sound as it hit.

Doug, always the clown, fell over backward into the snow.

This was our cue to really let him have it.

In seconds we were bombarding one another with snowballs. We were making and tossing them too quickly to be accurate. But about one in five hit its target.

Shannon and I teamed up against Doug and Red. Doug busily stockpiled snowballs, stacking them up in front of him. Red tossed his wildly, not even bothering to pack them tightly enough to travel far. Half the snow blew back in his face.

"Bull's-eye!"

Shannon hit Red right in the forehead with a beauty.

"Hey—no iceballs!" he cried, rubbing his forehead, which was bright red.

"That's not an iceball. I just have a powerful throw!" Shannon shouted.

We were laughing and having a great time when Lou surprised us by poking his head out the barn door. We'd thought he was in the house. "I had some chores to do," he called to us. "The Jeep's in here. Pile your stuff into it. I'll get the keys from the house and be right out."

I heaved one last snowball at Doug. It only missed him by about three feet. Okay, okay. I haven't got the best arm in the world. I'm a scientist. Not an athlete. "Shannon and I win!" I cried and started for the house, very pleased that it was time to go.

"You win?" Doug shouted. "How? By taking the most hits?"

Shannon picked up a handful of snow and shoved it into his face. They started to wrestle around, and she went sliding onto her back into a deep snowdrift.

"Okay, okay. It's a tie," she said, rolling out of the way as Doug tried to cover her with an armload of snow.

"Hey—come on, let's get going," I said. "Look—it's getting ready to snow again."

They all looked up. Heavy-looking dark clouds had completely covered the blue sky.

I suddenly realized I was cold and wet. My cheeks burned. I tried to feel my nose with my gloved hand. I felt nothing.

We grabbed our bags from the kitchen and carried them to the barn. It was only a little warmer inside the barn. The ground was hard and covered with straw.

The air was heavy and sweet smelling. Red found a switch and turned on a long fluorescent light attached to one of the rafters.

As the gray-blue light flickered on, the Jeep came into view. I don't think I was ever so glad to see a vehicle of any kind!

"Hey, look—a snowmobile!" Doug said, pointing to the back wall of the barn.

"Forget it," Shannon said, tugging the sleeve of Doug's coat. "Playtime is over, Doug. We've got to hit the road."

Outside, the wind had picked up and the sky was even darker.

Even if we make it to town, I thought, will we be able to start for home before we're completely snowed in again?

I tried not to think like that.

I started to toss my bag into the back of the Jeep when something caught my eye. "Hey—look at the license plate," I said to Red. "It's from Alabama—not Vermont."

"So?" He gave me a funny look.

"Well, why does Lou have Alabama plates on his car if he lives in Vermont?"

"A lot of people buy their cars out of state to save on taxes," Red said. He stared at the Alabama plate on the back of the Jeep. "But you're right, Ariel. It *is* a little strange."

"Who cares?" Doug said impatiently. "We're getting out of here. That's all that counts."

"Hey—here comes Lou," I said.

We watched him hurrying from the house in a jacket that did fit him, zipping it as he walked, keeping his head down and out of the gusting wind. He stepped into the barn and stamped the snow off his workboots. "Whoooeeee! It's cold!"

He was standing close enough for me to smell the beer on his breath. It's not even lunchtime, I thought, and he's already started to drink.

Oh, who cares? I scolded myself. In a short while we'll be rid of him. We'll never have to see him again.

"All right. Everybody pile in," he said, pulling open the door on the driver's side. "It's going to be a tight squeeze." He turned to Shannon. "Why don't you squeeze in next to me, Sweetcakes?"

I could see that Doug had had enough. He started toward Lou, fury in his dark eyes.

I quickly pulled him back, holding on to his arm. "Doug—no—we're going now," I whispered.

I turned Doug toward the Jeep and gave him a shove. We all piled in. Lou was right about it being a bit snug. The Jeep was only supposed to hold four, not five, people—and a load of bags. Shannon solved the problem by sitting next to me on Doug's lap. Somehow we all fit. We were uncomfortable, but no one was complaining. We were too happy to be leaving.

"Quite a load we got here," Lou said, fumbling in his jacket pocket for the key. "But we might make it as far as the bottom of the drive!" He thought this was a hilarious joke, and he laughed long and hard, slapping the steering wheel, not caring that the rest of us were silent.

He slid the key in the ignition, put his foot on the clutch and the gearshift in neutral, and turned the key.

Nothing.

Silence.

"That's strange," Lou said, making a face.

"Is it in neutral?" Red asked from the front passenger seat.

"Yeah. Of course it's in neutral," Lou said sharply. "I'm not as dumb as you look, you know."

"Try it again," Red said, ignoring Lou's flaring temper.

Lou turned the key and pressed down hard on the gas pedal.

Still nothing.

Not a whine. Not a cough.

Just silence. Unbearably silent silence!

"You don't have to push on the gas. It's fuel injected," Red said softly.

"Listen, Carrot Head, you don't have to tell me how to drive my own car," Lou snapped.

"Maybe the gearshift froze," Red said. "That happens sometimes. Try jiggling it."

Lou scowled and slapped the steering wheel angrily. But then he did follow Red's suggestion.

He turned the key.

The engine sputtered, then died.

"Do you believe this?" Lou shouted angrily, staring up through the windshield at the barn rafters. "Do you *believe* this? It's dead! Completely dead!"

Furious, he shoved open the door, stepped down to the ground, slammed the door behind him, and went storming toward the house, leaving us sitting in silence in the useless Jeep.

We piled out and saw that it had begun snowing again. It was really coming down.

We're trapped, I told myself. We are trapped. Really trapped. This time I couldn't talk myself out of it.

chapter

9

Doug poked at the fire, turning over a log. Flames leapt up with a roar. "That's more like it," he said, the firelight flickering in his dark brown eyes.

Shannon and I stood in front of the fire, allowing it to warm us. I rubbed my nose. It was starting to get a little feeling back.

"Where's Red?" Shannon asked, hugging herself, rubbing the sleeves of her heavy wool sweater.

"He's still in the barn," Doug said, carefully placing another log on the fire.

"What's he doing out there?" I asked, surprised.

"Tinkering with the Jeep, I guess." Doug picked up the poker and pushed the new log over the biggest flames. "Lou said he could fiddle with it all he likes. Red is sure he can get it to start."

"Shouldn't you be out there helping him?" Shannon asked.

"What can I do? I don't know anything about cars," Doug admitted, for once not being Mr. Macho. He put down the poker and walked over to the big window that faced the front. "It sure is coming down," he continued, shaking his head. "We could get another foot or two if it keeps up like this."

"Have the snowplows been through?" I asked.

He stared out into the gray for a while, trying to see down to the road. "No. No sign of them," he said, his back to us still.

"Maybe they don't ever plow this road at all," Shannon said glumly.

"That's looking on the bright side," I joked.

Feeling a little warmer, I backed away from the fire and sat down on the couch.

"Well, we'll be out of here by spring," Doug said, walking over to the glass case in the corner, looking at the guns admiringly.

"You have a lousy sense of humor," Shannon muttered, only half teasing.

"Well, what can we do?" Doug snapped. "Fly home? You want to fly home? We've tried everything we could—haven't we?"

"Stop yelling," Shannon said, making a disgusted face. "I hate it when you yell like that."

"I wasn't yelling. I just don't see why you have to start giving me a hard time," Doug said, still examining the gunrack. "Maybe you'd rather spend your time with Lou. I think you two make a great couple."

Things were getting pretty tense. "Hey—I just

remembered something," I said, straightening up on the couch, excited by my thought.

Shannon and Doug, ready to escalate their argument, turned to look at me instead.

"What about the snowmobile?" I asked. "You know, the one we saw in the barn. Someone could ride that to town and call our parents and get us help and everything."

"No way, babe," a voice said behind us.

I turned to see that Lou had come in from the kitchen. "That thing hasn't worked in years. It's just junk." He took a swig from the beer can in his hand.

"Oh," I said, disappointed. "Back to the drawing board, I guess."

"Is Mr. Fixit still trying to get that Jeep to run?" Lou asked, slurring his words.

"Yeah, I guess," Doug said.

"I think the fuel line is frozen," Lou said. He chuckled for some reason. "I knew a guy who froze to death in his car once," he continued, a smile forming under his dark, scraggly beard.

Oh no. Not another one of his gruesome stories, I thought, rolling my eyes.

But the story seemed to be over. It was a one-sentence anecdote. I hoped.

No such luck.

"Crazy guy," Lou muttered, staring at his beer can. "He was stiff as a board. And bright blue. Blue as a baboon!" Lou started to laugh.

He stopped abruptly and walked over to the phone.

He picked up the receiver and listened. "Hey! How about that!"

"Is it working?" I cried, jumping up off the couch eagerly.

"Gotcha!" he said, grinning at me. He replaced the receiver, laughing even harder. "It ain't fixed, Blondie. But it's crackling a bit," he said. "That means they're working on it. Should be fixed soon." He turned his attention to Shannon, eyeing her hungrily.

I glanced at my watch. It was almost one o'clock. Outside it was almost dark enough to be night.

Lou belched loudly. "Anybody want lunch?" he asked. He finished the beer and crushed the can in his hand. "Just sandwiches. Make 'em yourself, okay? With you clowns eating everything but the wallpaper, we're running a little low on supplies."

Suddenly I thought of Eva. And I realized that she hadn't come downstairs yet.

"Eva—" I started. "Is Eva down yet, Lou?"

But he had returned to the kitchen, most likely to get another beer.

"I'm starving," Doug said, leaning the poker against the fireplace. "Let's go make sandwiches and eat them in front of the fire."

"We should call Red in," Shannon said, following Doug to the kitchen.

"I'll be there in a minute," I said, not moving.

I had this bad feeling about Eva. I remembered what Red had told me about the fight he had heard the night before, how she and Lou had argued. How it had gotten so quiet after Lou had hit her.

74

I glanced up at the gunrack Doug had been admiring. So many guns.

Just how violent a guy was Lou?

Just how dangerous could he be?

Now here it was one o'clock. Lunchtime, and Eva still hadn't come downstairs.

I had this feeling, this bad feeling.

I just had to go up and make sure Eva was okay.

I crept up the stairs. There was no need to be quiet, really. But I went up as silently as I could, the wooden steps creaking lightly under my stocking feet.

I walked up to Eva's bedroom at the head of the narrow balcony corridor. The door was closed. I stopped outside and listened.

I could hear Lou downstairs in the kitchen, talking to Doug and Shannon. I guessed the kitchen was right beneath this part of the balcony.

I pressed my ear against the bedroom door. It was silent inside.

I knocked quietly. Once, twice.

No sound inside.

I knocked a little louder.

Come on, Eva. Wake up. Say something.

"Eva?" I called, my face right up to the door.

No reply.

"Eva? Are you awake?"

I heard Lou laughing loudly about something down in the kitchen. Probably another one of his disgusting stories, I thought.

"Eva?"

Silence in the bedroom.

I took a deep breath, turned the brass doorknob, and pushed open the door.

"Eva?"

It was stuffy and warm in the bedroom. In the gray light from the uncurtained window, I could see her on the bed. She was sprawled on her back, her head off the pillow, her eyes open, unmoving.

"Oh my God!" I heard myself cry.

chapter
10

Eva blinked and started to pull herself up, staring at me, confused.

I guess my scream woke her up.

I felt like a total fool. But the way she had been lying with her head bent at such a strange angle and her eyes wide open made me jump to the wrong conclusion.

"What?" she asked, her voice choked with sleep.

"I—uh— Sorry I s-screamed," I stammered. "It's just that—your eyes were wide open and—"

"Sometimes I sleep with my eyes open," she said, still acting bewildered as if she didn't know where she was or who I was.

I could see a big red bruise on her right cheek. The cheek was all swollen. Her right eye only opened halfway.

"I'm sorry—" I repeated, taking a step back toward the door.

"You shouldn't be here," she said, her voice a hoarse whisper.

"What?" I wasn't sure I had heard her correctly.

"You shouldn't be here," she repeated, a little more loudly, a little more forcefully. "Please . . ." She didn't sound angry—it was almost as if she were pleading with me.

I got all flustered. I could feel my face turning red. I backed up right into the doorknob, then turned and escaped into the hall, pulling the door closed behind me.

It was much cooler in the hall. I stood there outside Eva's bedroom door for a few seconds, waiting to calm down, waiting for my breathing to return to normal.

"You shouldn't be here."

What did Eva mean?

Did she mean I shouldn't be in her bedroom? Or did she mean that the four of us shouldn't be in this house?

Why did she look so frightened? Was it just because I had startled her when I screamed and woke her up?

No. I had the feeling that she was trying to warn me.

"You shouldn't be here."

Well, I thought, leaning against the balcony railing, I'd *love* to get away, Eva. I can't *wait* to get away, to leave this house and never come back, and my friends feel exactly the same way.

But we're trapped here. We *can't* leave.

I looked down into the living room. The fire was

still blazing. Doug and Shannon were carrying their lunch plates to the couch in front of the fireplace. Through the window I could see the snow still falling, large, heavy flakes, being swirled in all directions by the blowing wind.

I took a deep breath and let it out. I couldn't get rid of the nervous feeling I had.

Maybe a sandwich will help, I thought.

I walked downstairs, Eva's sleep-filled voice still in my mind, and headed for the kitchen. Lou was leaning against the island counter, staring out the back window at the falling snow, another can of beer in his hand.

He turned when he heard me enter the room. "Hey, Dollface. Look at it coming down. I think your friend Red is wasting his time out there. If he doesn't come in soon, we'll have to send a rescue party." He was beginning to slur his words. His eyes looked very red and watery.

"I-I'm just going to make a sandwich," I said.

"Whatever," he muttered.

He walked over to the wall phone and picked up the receiver. After listening for a few seconds, his face turned bright red and his eyes bulged in fury. "Still not fixed!" he bellowed. He tossed down his beer can, grabbed the phone with both hands, and pulled it right out of the wall.

I didn't say anything. I didn't know what to do. He was obviously out of control.

I guess he saw how frightened I was. He stared at me

79

for a long moment, then averted his eyes. After dropping the phone on the counter, he left the kitchen.

I slapped together a sandwich of some kind from the stuff that was left out on the counter. I didn't even see what I was putting in it. Then I hurried to the living room to rejoin Doug and Shannon.

I wished Red would come in from the barn. Somehow I knew I'd feel safer if all four of us were together—especially with Lou acting so crazy. And Doug eager to have it out with Lou.

Again I saw the swollen, red bruise on Eva's face. And then I saw Lou tearing the phone off the wall in a rage.

It isn't safe here, I realized. It isn't safe here because of Lou.

We have to be very careful. Very careful not to give Lou any reason to turn his anger on us.

"Hey—where'd you go?" Shannon asked as I sat down in the armchair near the fireplace across from her and Doug.

"Upstairs. To Eva's room," I whispered. I made sure that Lou wasn't nearby. Then I told them what had happened upstairs, and what Eva had said to me.

"You probably just scared her, screaming like that," Doug said.

"Maybe," I said.

"Yeah, Doug's right," Shannon said quickly.

But I could tell from their voices that they were just as troubled as I was.

The afternoon dragged on. We kept feeding the fire,

staring at the bright orange flames, listening to it crackle. Eva came downstairs after a while, muttered a greeting, and disappeared into the kitchen.

Outside, the wind howled and the snow continued to come down. I stared out the window for a while, watching the trees sway and bend under the weight of the snow.

We found a deck of cards and played hearts for a while. But none of us was really into it. It took us three games to realize that four cards were missing from the deck.

It was late afternoon when I glanced up from the armchair and saw someone outside staring into the window.

"Oh! Look!" I cried, startled.

His face was completely covered by a blue ski mask.

He leaned close to the window, so close that his breath fogged the glass.

But even through the fogged-up window I could see that he was staring right at me!

chapter
11

I sat there staring back at him for a few moments.

"Who's *that?*" Shannon cried.

Without thinking, I leapt up from the chair and ran to the window.

The pane was still fogged from the stranger's breath. But he was gone.

I stood on tiptoe, pressing my head against the glass, trying to see around to the sides of the house. But there was no one there now.

"He's gone," I said.

"How?" Doug was right behind me.

"He just disappeared. Look—the footprints stop a few feet from the window."

"Weird!" Doug said. He pushed me out of the way to get a better look.

"He looked so scary in that ski mask," Shannon said. "Like someone in a horror movie."

"But who could it be?" I asked.

"Weird," Doug repeated. He wasn't being terribly helpful.

"If someone had walked here in the snow, why wouldn't he knock on the door?" Shannon asked, sounding as frightened as I felt.

"Yeah. Why did he just stare at us like that?" Doug asked.

"Good question," I said, my heart still pounding.

"Hey—what's happening?" Lou called down from the balcony.

I jumped at the sound of his voice. I hadn't realized that he was upstairs.

"Someone was outside," I called up to him.

"What?"

"Someone in a ski mask. He was just staring at us through the window," I said.

Lou started down the stairs. He laughed. "You've had more beers than me—right?"

"No, Lou. We really saw him," Doug said, still at the window.

Suddenly Red appeared on the balcony, pulling a sweater over his head. I hadn't noticed him come into the house. "What's going on?" His face was bright red, from being out in the cold barn for so long.

"Your wacko pals here saw a snowman in a ski mask," Lou said, chuckling.

"There *was* someone outside," I said.

"And he didn't come to the door?" Red asked.

"They've gone snow-blind or something," Lou said, plopping down in the armchair by the fireplace. "Or maybe they've been staring into the fire too long. They're hallucinating. Seeing ghosts."

"Give us a break, Lou," Doug said impatiently. "We're not crazy. There was someone at the window."

"Hey, Mr. Fixit—any luck with the Jeep?" Lou asked, ignoring Doug.

Red came down the stairs, his eyes on me. "No. No luck. I can't find the trouble. I'm totally stumped."

"The phone'll be fixed soon," Lou said. "We'll call the garage in town first thing." He cursed. "At least that phone better be fixed! Whoooo, that makes me mad. You see what I did to that sucker in the kitchen? I tore it clean off!" He tossed back his head and whooped with laughter.

None of us joined in. It made me really nervous to see Lou lose control.

Red shivered as he walked up close to the fire. "Wow. This feels good," he said, holding his hands up close to the flames. "I am *frozen*. I don't think my fingers will ever move again!"

"Hey—Eva—move your buns! Put on a pot of coffee! The boy is freezing—ya hear?" Lou yelled.

"Doesn't anybody care about the guy we saw in a ski mask?" Doug asked Lou.

"Maybe it was Jack Frost," Lou said, rolling his eyes. "Or Santa Claus, thinking this was the North Pole." Again he threw back his head and laughed up at the cathedral ceiling. That really cracked him up.

Doug just stood in the middle of the room looking frustrated and annoyed.

"Hey, turkey, you've got a pretty good build," Lou said suddenly to Doug.

"What?" Doug stared at him.

"You work out?" Lou asked.

"Yeah. A little," Doug said, obviously suspicious of Lou's sudden interest in him. "I'm on the wrestling team at school. I was All-State last year."

"Yeah?" Lou stood up and took a few steps toward Doug. "You're pretty good, huh?"

"Well, I don't work at it that much," Doug admitted. "But I'm kind of a natural athlete, I guess."

Good old modest Doug.

Lou stepped up and squeezed the biceps on Doug's right arm with both hands. I think he squeezed pretty hard because Doug flinched.

"Not bad. Not bad," Lou said, grinning, his face a few inches from Doug's face. "There's some muscle somewhere under that flab."

"Thanks," Doug said sarcastically.

"I used to be a wrestler too," Lou said, rubbing his beard, checking Doug out. "I used to be pretty good. Before I got this." He patted his beer belly. "How about a match?"

Doug's mouth dropped open. "Huh? Right here?"

"Over there," Lou said, pointing behind the couch. "We'll move this shaggy white rug over. Come on, Hulkster. How about it? Let's see what you've got."

"Well . . ."

I knew Doug was going to do it. There was no way

macho Doug would ever turn down a challenge. And he'd been dying to get at Lou, to pay Lou back for coming on to Shannon.

"You chicken or what?" Lou said, challenging Doug, poking him playfully in the chest. "Cluck-cluck-cluck." Lou began flapping his arms and clucking at the top of his voice.

Don't do it, Doug, I prayed silently to myself. Just walk away. Don't do it.

"No, I'm not chicken," Doug said. "It's just that you haven't practiced for a while, right? You're kind of out of shape. And I don't—"

"Cluck-cluck-cluck! The Hulkster is lookin' for excuses!" Lou bellowed and dragged the rug over behind the sofa. "You don't want to hurt me? Come on, turkey." He walked onto the white rug. "Let an old dude give you a few pointers."

"Lou—what are you doing?" Eva came in from the kitchen.

"Nothing you'd be interested in," Lou snapped. "Leave us alone."

"But, Lou—these kids—"

"Shut your yap, Eva," Lou shouted impatiently. "Before I shut it for you." He glared at her. She shrank back. "We're just having a little fun, trying to make the time pass. Right, Hulkster?"

Doug pulled off his sweater and straightened the long-sleeved pullover he was wearing under it. Then he stepped onto the rug and faced Lou. "Okay," he said. "Let's go."

Eva sighed loudly to show her displeasure and

returned to the kitchen. Shannon and I stood by the couch at the edge of the rug. Red watched from the fireplace, a tight frown on his face.

Doug, how can you do this? I wondered silently. This can only lead to trouble. Please, please—don't get Lou more worked up than he already is.

"Anytime you're ready," Doug said.

"Go easy on me, okay?" Lou said in a wimpy little voice, holding his hands together as if he were praying. Then he got into a wrestling position, leaning forward, pressing both hands against his knees, moving from side to side. "Come on. Show me something, chicken lips. Show me something!"

The match started out very playfully. Doug moved first, grabbing Lou's left leg, pulling him to the rug, then gripping his arms behind him.

Both Doug and Lou seemed to be having fun, rolling around on the white rug, putting different holds on each other, groaning and grunting like professional wrestlers.

Shannon started to get into it, yelling a bit, cheering Doug on. Even I relaxed some since they just seemed to be horsing around.

Doug was doing really well. He kept putting holds on Lou and getting Lou down on his back. He was pretty much in control the whole time.

Then Doug pinned Lou, pressing his shoulders onto the rug. "One—two—three!" Doug counted, out of breath. He released Lou and jumped to his feet. "That's the match," Doug said, smiling at Shannon.

Doug started to walk away, but Lou reached out and

grabbed his leg. Lou's face was bright red. His forehead was covered in sweat, and he was breathing hard. "Hey, Hulkster—we're not done," he said and he didn't sound playful anymore.

"Hey, Lou—" Red called from the fire, looking worried.

But Lou pulled Doug down to the rug, grabbed his arms, and cursing loudly, tried to bend him backward. "Ow—hey!" Doug cried.

"We're not done," Lou repeated through clenched teeth.

This was no longer a casual little match. Lou wasn't playing for fun anymore.

He began wrestling wildly, grabbing Doug's arms, shoving him hard into the rug, banging his head on the floor.

"We're not done!"

"Lou—stop!" Red called, running over.

"Ow!" Doug screamed in pain as Lou grabbed his leg with both hands and pulled it back.

"Ow!"

"Doug! Are you okay?" Shannon cried.

Red grabbed Lou by the shoulder and tried to yank him off Doug.

"My leg! I heard it crack!" Doug cried, his face twisted in pain and panic.

Red pulled Lou away. Lou climbed quickly to his feet, breathing heavily, noisily. He stared down at Doug, bewildered. "Hey—what happened, sports fans?"

Doug's face had gone as white as the rug. He

grabbed his knee with both hands. "I—I think it's broken!"

"Huh?" Lou cried. "I was just playing, big fella. I couldn't have broken it."

"I don't believe this! I don't believe this!" Shannon was screaming hysterically, her hands up to her face.

I bent down and pulled Doug's hands away from his knee. "Let me see it," I said. "I studied a little bit about knees for that science project last term."

"It's all right," Lou said, leaning over me, still breathing noisily, gasping for air. "I didn't hardly touch him."

I could smell the beer on his breath. "Come on, Lou. Back away, please," I said. "You're blocking the light."

"Whooooo—the little lady takes charge! Okay, okay. I can take a hint." He took a step back.

I rolled up the leg of Doug's jeans.

"Oww," Doug howled.

"Try to move it," I said. "Try to bend it."

"It'll bend," Lou insisted. "No way I broke it. We were just having fun—right, Hulkster?"

Doug made a face as he moved the leg.

"It's bending," I said. "Do it again."

He bent the knee again.

"How's it feel?" I asked, checking the ligaments.

"Better," he said.

"I knew it," Lou said. "I was just playing, you know. If I really wanted to hurt him, I could've."

"It's not broken," I said. "Nothing seems to be torn. Guess you just sprained it."

"Thanks, Doc," Doug said gratefully.

"Hey, carrot head, it was an accident," Lou insisted to Red. "Don't give me any of your looks, or I'll get *you* on the mat next. I'd just *sit* on you! Ha-ha!"

"Come on, Lou. How about a cup of coffee?" Red said softly. He started to lead Lou into the kitchen.

"Yeah. Good idea," Lou said. "Some caffeine. Come on, sports fans. Who else wants coffee?" He lurched into the kitchen, leaning unsteadily on Red.

A few seconds later Red came hurrying back, a worried look on his face.

Shannon and I were helping Doug to his feet. Doug was taking a few tender steps, trying out his knee.

Red ran up to me, leaned close, and whispered loud enough for all of us to hear. "Your room, Ariel. In five minutes, okay? We've got to get out of here—*now!*"

chapter
12

*R*ed made some excuse to Lou, and a few minutes later the four of us were hunkered down in my little bedroom, Shannon, Doug, and me sitting around the edges of the bed, Red pacing back and forth by the window.

It was only a little after six o'clock, but it was dark as midnight. The wind howled, rattling the pane of glass in the wooden window. The lights flickered for a few seconds, but didn't go out.

I was feeling really nervous, wondering why Red wanted us to meet so urgently. My hands were ice cold. I slid them under the quilt.

"He deliberately tried to hurt me. I know it," Doug was saying, leaning forward to massage his knee.

"He got carried away," Red said. "He totally lost it, Doug. I don't think he knew *what* he was doing."

"He knew all right," Doug muttered bitterly.

"He is crazy," Red agreed. "And dangerous. We have to get out of here—now."

"Huh?" Shannon cried, glancing out the window.

"I'm serious," Red said. "We have no choice."

"But, Red," I said, climbing to my feet. "Look outside. It's dark already."

"It's dark, but it's stopped snowing," Red answered. "Listen, guys, we don't have to go far. We can find the next town. Or just find another house. But we've *got* to get away from this place—right now!"

"What's the rush?" Shannon asked.

Red raised his finger to his lips, motioning for her to talk more quietly. He walked over to the bedroom door to make sure it was closed.

"Yeah. What's the rush?" Doug repeated sullenly, still massaging his leg. "Lou's an obnoxious jerk. But at least it's warm here and there's food and stuff."

"He's not just a jerk," Red said in a loud whisper. "He's *really* dangerous, Doug. He's going to rob us and then leave us here with no way to escape."

"What?" all three of us cried at once.

Again Red motioned frantically for us to be quiet.

"How do you know that?" I asked. The quilt wasn't helping. My hands weren't warming up. In fact, I felt cold all over.

"I heard him," Red said, stuffing his hands into his jeans pockets. "I heard him talking to Eva. I was up here in my room. Next to their room. I was getting an extra sweater just before the big wrestling match."

Doug groaned.

"The two of them were in their bedroom. I could hear every word Lou said. He talks so loud, and the walls are real thin. He said he was going to wait till later tonight. Then he was going to rob us and pull out all the phones and leave."

"Eva's in on it too?" I asked, not quite ready to believe what Red was saying.

"No. She tried to argue with him," Red whispered.

"She seems like a nice person," Shannon said. "I don't know how she got stuck with him."

"Same way you got stuck with me," Doug muttered darkly, then laughed.

"You're not so bad," Shannon said, patting him on the shoulder. Then she quickly added, "Compared to Lou."

"I think that's what Lou and Eva were arguing about last night," Red said. "She tried to talk him out of his plan, and he hit her."

"So she tried arguing with him again this afternoon?" I asked.

"Yeah. But she didn't get anywhere. He just cursed a blue streak and stormed out into the hall. That was about when you saw the guy in the blue ski mask."

"Yeah. Who *was* that guy anyway?" Doug asked.

"And why did Lou want to pretend he didn't exist?" I asked.

"Maybe the guy in the blue ski mask is in on this with Lou," Red suggested. Then he added, "I just want to make sure we're out of here before they can carry out their plans."

A loud cracking noise startled us all.

"What was *that?*" Shannon cried.

"Just snow falling off the roof," I said, my heart beating fast. "This place is definitely giving me the creeps."

"Wait here. I want to show you something else," Red said, walking quickly out of the room. We heard him go down the hall. A few seconds later he reappeared.

"Look what I found shoved in my bottom dresser drawer," he said. He held up two photographs in Plexiglas frames. They were enlarged snapshots of a man and woman. The couple appeared to be in their thirties. The woman was dark haired, small, and rather plain. The man was much taller, lean and angular, with a mop of curly, black hair on top of his smiling face.

"Who are they?" Shannon asked, confused.

"That's what *I'd* like to know," Red whispered, setting the photographs down on top of the dresser. "Who are they? And why were their photos shoved into an empty dresser drawer?"

"What's the big deal?" I asked, not understanding Red's concern. "So someone shoved some old photos into a drawer. So what?"

"There's something strange going on here," Red whispered, glancing at the door. "Downstairs in the living room, I saw places on the mantel where these photos had been."

"How could you tell that?" Doug asked skeptically.

"From the dust," Red replied, still whispering. "The house hasn't been dusted in a long time. I could tell. But there was no dust in the spots where those pictures had been. That means they were recently removed and hidden in my dresser."

"You mean—" Shannon started.

"I mean Lou must have hidden those photos. For some reason."

"Let me see those pictures. Those people look kind of familiar to me," I said.

"Do you think Lou did something to them?" Shannon asked, her face filled with fear.

"Maybe they're just away," I said quickly.

"Maybe," Red agreed. "But maybe this isn't Lou and Eva's house."

"Well, that would explain the tea," I said.

"Huh?" Doug turned to look at me, confused.

"When I asked Eva for a cup of tea last night, she had to search all the cabinets to find the tea bags."

"Because it isn't her house," Red said, grateful for proof of his theory.

"And that jacket Lou wore yesterday," I said thinking hard. "It was way too small on him. He could hardly fasten it."

"It wasn't his jacket?" Doug asked.

"Right," Red said.

"This *is* scary," Shannon said softly.

"Well, what are they doing here if this isn't their place?" Doug asked.

"Maybe they know that couple—the owners. Maybe they have permission to be here," Shannon said. I was glad she was trying to think positive for once. But I knew she wasn't on target.

"Then why would Lou hide the photographs?" I asked.

"Ariel's right," Red said.

"Who cares about that stuff?" Doug said impatiently. "You heard Lou planning to rob us and leave us here—right?"

"Right," Red said, turning his gaze out the window.

"Well, what more do we need to know?" Doug cried, jumping up in spite of his bad knee. "We have no choice. We have to get away from here."

"But how?" Shannon asked, her hands clasped so tightly together in her lap that her knuckles were white.

"I've taken care of that," Red said, a grin spreading across his face. He reached into his jeans pocket and pulled out a set of keys. "The Jeep," he said.

"We take the Jeep?" Shannon cried.

"You said it was still busted," Doug said.

"I lied," Red told him, motioning for us all to whisper.

"Huh?"

"I got it going this afternoon. It was simple. I just had to clear the fuel line. I was going to tell Lou it was fixed. But then I heard him arguing with Eva about robbing us, so I decided to hold on to the keys and tell him it was still frozen."

"That's great!" Doug cried. "We can drive it right out of here!"

"If we can get out of the house without him hearing us," Red said, his expression darkening. "That's the part I'm afraid of."

96

"Well, if he catches us sneaking out, we'll just—" Doug said. But he couldn't think of what we would do.

"If he catches us, there's no telling what he might do," Red said, nervously raking his wavy hair with one hand. "He's been drinking all day, and I think he's a violent guy."

"Tell me about it," Doug said, rubbing his knee.

"You think he might try to hurt us?" I asked.

"Ssshhh!" Red whispered suddenly. He raised a hand, motioning for us not to move.

We all froze.

It was so silent I thought I could hear the blood pumping through my veins.

There were footsteps on the back stairs. Lou or Eva. Were they going to come in?

No. Whoever it was walked right past my room.

"We'll have to wait till they go to sleep," Red whispered, staring at me for some reason. "Then we'll sneak out and take the Jeep."

"Why can't we leave right now?" Doug asked, more of a challenge than a question. "Why do we have to sit through dinner with him?"

"Yes. I agree," Shannon said quietly, looking really scared.

"We won't get out the door. He'll hear us," Red said.

"Red's right," I agreed. "Let Lou have six or seven more beers. By ten or so, he'll be out like a light. Then we can get away easily."

Doug reluctantly agreed.

* * *

A short while later we trooped down to dinner. It was pretty tense, knowing what Lou had planned and what *we* had planned. No one could think of anything much to say. Lou kept eyeing us suspiciously, but he didn't say much either. He grumbled about the phone and about the snow. I was glad to see that he was downing beer after beer.

He'll be sound asleep before ten, I thought. Then we'll be on our way.

But I underestimated Lou. He didn't stumble upstairs until nearly midnight. We had all gone upstairs before nine-thirty. We were all packed and ready to leave. Then we just waited, waited, waited.

It was nearly twelve-thirty when we decided to risk moving out. "We'll take the back stairs," Red whispered, leading the way.

"What do we say if we're caught?" Shannon asked, looking frightened.

"We wanted a little fresh air?" Doug suggested.

Shannon shoved him impatiently. "Not funny."

"We'll have to deal with that when it happens," Red said grimly. Then he added, "Let's hope it doesn't happen."

We edged out into the hallway, walking silently, carefully. Luckily the narrow hall was carpeted. Our boots didn't make a sound as we headed toward the back stairs.

I can't believe we're doing this, I thought. I can't believe any of this is happening to me. This was supposed to be a fun ski weekend. How can we be sneaking out of a house, trying to escape from a dangerous lunatic who means to rob us, about to steal a Jeep to try to drive through the heaviest snow I'd ever seen!

We're going to do it, I told myself.

We're going to get away.

We're going home.

Home.

I realized I hadn't thought about my parents all day.

Boy, will I be glad to see them, I thought.

If I ever see them again.

We walked slowly so we didn't make a sound and finally reached the back stairs.

Doug stopped on the top step. "Our coats," he whispered to Red. "They're by the front door."

"We'll have to go through the living room and get them, then go back to the kitchen," Red whispered.

If Lou came out of his room and looked down from the balcony, he'd see us.

But what choice did we have?

We started down the stairs, Doug first, followed by Red, then Shannon, then me.

To our horror the wooden stairs creaked with each footstep.

Had Lou heard us?

chapter
13

*T*he stairs groaned.

We sounded like stampeding elephants to me.

My heart stopped. I couldn't breathe. We all froze and glanced back up toward the hall.

Had Lou heard us? Was he coming after us?

There was no light from the end of the hall. The only light came from the bedroom lamp I had forgotten to switch off. No sign of Lou. No one moving among the shadows.

Below us the back of the house lay in darkness.

We continued our trek down the noisy stairs. I don't think any of us took a breath. I know I didn't.

I didn't breathe until I reached the back hall at the bottom of the stairs. But I knew we weren't out of the woods yet. We still had to get our coats from the front alcove, sneak back to the kitchen, steal out to the barn, and make our getaway in the Jeep without Lou stopping us.

It seemed impossible. Hopeless.

Just take it one step at a time, Ariel, I told myself. One step at a time.

When you're in a total panic, you don't care if your advice to yourself is a cliché or not.

We didn't say a word to one another. Our eyes did all the talking for us. We kept looking at one another, as if we had found a new, silent way to communicate.

Silently we crept through the narrow back passageway, into the front hall, and then into the living room. I could see only blackness out the big window. Across the room the fire had burned down to a pile of crackling, purple embers. The desk lamp on the phone table, the only light in the room, cast a yellow cone onto the white shag rug.

Holding my breath, I tiptoed to the phone and picked up the receiver.

Please, please be fixed.

If we could just call the police, we wouldn't have to go through with this.

No. No dial tone. Just loud crackling.

With a dispirited sigh, I replaced the receiver and followed my three friends across the room to the coat alcove.

"Maybe we should just slip out the front door," Shannon whispered, pulling on her down jacket. Our coats were still damp from our snowball fight that morning. Damp and cold. "Then we won't have to double back across the living room."

"Okay," Red said, patting her shoulder. He pulled his wool cap down over his head. "Of course that means we'll have to walk all around the house in the snow."

"No problem," Doug said, heading to the front door as he zipped up his coat. "The sooner we get outside, the better."

We all agreed. Somehow I felt that getting out of the house was ninety percent of the battle. I pulled on my mittens, also damp still, and followed them to the front door, glancing nervously up to the balcony.

Nothing moving up there.

No sign of Lou.

Red grabbed the front doorknob and started to open the door. Then he stopped and turned back into the room.

"The gunrack," he said, looking over to it in the corner near the fireplace.

"What about it?" Doug whispered.

"The guns are loaded, right?" Red whispered. "We might as well take one, just in case Lou does come after us."

"Take a gun?" I whispered. The thought made a cold chill run down my back.

"We wouldn't use it," Red said. "Chances are, we won't need it at all. But I really want to get away from here."

"Me too," Doug said enthusiastically. "That's a great idea, Red. I'll go get one."

He started across the room, walking almost normally, the pain in his knee having eased. But I hurried after him and grabbed the shoulder of his coat.

"No," I whispered. "We don't need it."

"Red's right," Doug insisted, pulling away from me. "We won't use it. But why take chances? Lou is crazy. You saw what he did to my leg."

He hurried eagerly to the gunrack, opened the glass door, and pulled a revolver down.

I stood in the middle of the floor, watching him, filled with a growing feeling of dread.

I hated guns. I hated being in the same room with guns.

I hated seeing Doug walking toward me with that loaded revolver in his gloved hand. And I hated the look on his face. The look that said, This is cool. This is exciting.

"Okay," Red whispered to Doug, glancing up at the still-silent balcony, "hold on to it till I get the Jeep started up. Then I'll take it from you."

"No problem," Doug said, examining the barrel. "I've handled a gun before."

I could tell he wasn't as confident as he pretended to be. I think we all could. But what difference did it make? We were about to escape. A few more seconds and we'd be out the door.

And still no Lou.

Maybe we can do it, I thought.

Maybe we can actually pull this off.

And won't Lou be surprised when he comes out of

his room in the morning and finds us all gone, and him stranded here without his Jeep, his dreadful plans ruined.

"Come on. Quick!" Red whispered.

He pulled open the front door and we stepped out into the night.

chapter
_____

14

T he shock of the sudden cold made me gasp. The temperature must have dropped twenty degrees since our snowball fight.

The winds had stopped. Everything seemed frozen, still. Even my breath froze in front of me as I followed the others around to the side of the house, my eyes slowly adjusting to the shifting shades of gray.

The top of the snow had hardened, and our boots crunched through it as we walked, breaking the surface with each step.

Walking as quickly and silently as we could over the frozen snow, we made our way to the back of the house and headed across the yard to the barn. My cheeks were stinging from the cold, and my eyes were watering. I felt as if I were seeing everything through a distorted glass, a distorted, dark glass.

I remembered that I had a flashlight in my pack. But

I quickly decided it wouldn't be a good idea to use it. Lou might look out from his bedroom window and see it.

None of us said a word. It was as if our voices had been frozen too. We walked in a straight line toward the barn. I found it easier to walk in Doug's deep footprints.

We were only a few yards from the barn when I turned around and looked back to the house. A yellowish light shone from one of the upstairs bedrooms. The shade was drawn. I couldn't tell if it was Lou's room or not.

Shivering, I turned back toward the barn. Doug and Red were struggling with the door. Doug had set the revolver down on the snow and was tugging hard on the large metal latch. Red was trying to pry the door open with his gloved hands.

"It's frozen stuck," Doug whispered.

"We can get it," Red whispered back. "We *have* to get it. Keep trying."

A raw wind came up suddenly, swirling at us from the direction of the house. It seemed to be blowing against us, keeping the barn door shut.

They pulled again, straining with all their strength. The door swung open a few inches and then stopped. Doug let go of the latch, and both boys wrapped their hands on the edge of the wooden door and pulled.

It moved. A little more. A little more.

Then it stuck again.

Doug frantically kicked the frozen snow out of the way. Then they tugged some more, leaning so far back as they pulled, it looked as if they might topple onto their backs into the snow.

Finally it was open wide enough to drive the Jeep through.

Both boys were breathing hard, their breath frozen, gray mists against the solid black sky.

"Come on. Hurry." Doug picked up the revolver, and the four of us stepped into the dark barn.

We heard creatures scampering as we entered. Probably mice. The inside of the barn was even darker than the backyard, but we didn't dare turn on the overhead light.

"Let's get to the Jeep," Red whispered.

It was so dark in there, I could barely make it out at the other end of the barn.

We took a couple of steps across the frozen dirt floor when the powerful wind slammed the door shut behind us.

"Ohh!" I let out a startled cry.

All four of us spun around, terrified.

The wind howled.

"No one there. Just the wind," Shannon said, sounding very relieved.

We stared at the door. We pushed it open again, until it stuck in the hard, frozen snow.

My heart was pounding. I felt cold all over. I don't think I ever knew what "chilled to the bone" meant until that moment.

"Maybe we should turn on the light," Shannon whispered.

"No need," Red said, leading the way through the

dark barn. "I have the keys in my hand. I can start the Jeep in the dark."

Behind us the wind blew hard against the open barn door. I stepped up close to Doug, close enough to see that even he looked scared.

We were just about in the center of the barn, our boots crunching loudly on the hard ground. Something fluttered above our heads.

"A bat?" I whispered to Doug.

"It isn't a butterfly," he cracked.

"Come on. Let's pile into the Jeep and bomb out of here!" I cried, straining to see what was fluttering above us.

When I moved my eyes back down, I saw a figure looming just in front of us.

A man was standing against a post, staring at us.

"It's Lou!" Shannon screamed, her terrified voice echoing off the high rafters.

"He's got a gun!" Red cried.

chapter
15

*E*verything seemed to disappear.

The barn.

The Jeep.

The cold.

Even the darkness.

All that existed was Lou, standing in front of us, blocking our path, staring at us, a dark metal object in his hand.

The loud explosion at my side made me jump.

But I didn't realize at first what it was.

It didn't sound like a gunshot. Not like the gunshots on TV.

It was much louder. It had so many echoes.

I stood staring at the dark figure, staring at Lou, and it took the longest time for me to realize that the loud explosion *had* been a gunshot.

And then I saw Lou drop to the ground.

He didn't make a sound. Just collapsed, toppling back, hitting the ground so hard, he bounced.

And then he lay still.

And then I slowly, slowly realized that Doug had shot him.

It all took so long to filter into my brain. As if I were in slow motion.

And I didn't even realize I was screaming, screaming at the top of my lungs, until Shannon stepped over and put her arm around me.

"I—I shot him." I think I heard Doug say that. I'm not really sure.

"I shot Lou, Red. Hey, Red—"

But Red wasn't there.

The fluorescent light on the rafter above us flickered on. The light seemed almost purple for some reason, then brightened to a blueish gray.

I turned around. Red stood by the lightswitch beside the open door.

"Red—I shot Lou!" Doug called to him, the revolver still in his hand. "I didn't mean to. I—"

Shannon was still holding on to me.

I was grateful she was there. I suddenly felt so dizzy, as if the sudden light had thrown me off-balance. Or was it the gunshot? I could still hear it echoing in the rafters.

Red came hurrying over, his frozen breath a cloud in front of him.

"It just went off," Doug said, staring at the gun in his hand. "I didn't think I squeezed the trigger, but I guess I did."

Red ran past him to kneel over the unmoving body on the floor. "Lou—" he started, then his voice choked.

Doug, Shannon, and I stepped forward, huddling together behind Red, staring down at Lou.

Except that it wasn't Lou.

It was another man, someone we'd never seen before.

Red pulled off his glove and held his hand up to the man's nostrils, then pressed his fingers against the man's throat.

"He's dead," Red said.

chapter

16

The man lay stiff, his eyes staring up at the rafters, arms straight at his sides, a small pistol on the ground beside his right hand.

He was wearing a thin, blue wool coat, no hat or gloves. He had a narrow face and a thick tuft of curly black hair. He looked to be in his late thirties, maybe early forties.

"He's dead. You killed him." Red turned his head to look up at Doug.

Doug's mouth dropped open in horror, in shock. He stared wide-eyed at the revolver in his hand, as if he had no idea how it had gotten there, or even what it was.

His mouth formed the word *no,* but no sound came out.

Red pulled open the man's coat. We could see the

hole in the shirt and coat made by the bullet and a smaller round tear in the chest, and a small dribble of blood.

"Who *is* he?" Shannon cried, averting her eyes, her voice tight and high-pitched.

"How can he be dead? I didn't even mean to shoot," Doug said.

"It was an accident," I said, putting a hand on Doug's shoulder, trying to soothe him.

Behind us the wind made the barn door creak and scrape against the hard snow. I shuddered.

Was this really happening?

Were we really in this freezing, creepy barn with a dead stranger on the floor? Had Doug really killed a man, a man none of us had ever seen before?

Then suddenly I realized I *had* seen him before.

"He's—he's the man—" I stammered, shivering too hard to get the words out.

"What?" Red asked, still bent over the body, checking for any sign of life.

"Don't you recognize him?" I cried. "He's the man in the photographs."

"Huh? What photographs?" Doug asked, his eyes still wild with fright, with disbelief.

"The photographs that were jammed into the dresser drawer. The man and the woman. He's the man."

"Ariel's right," Red said grimly, climbing to his feet. He pulled off his red ski hat. He was sweating despite the cold. "This is the guy, all right."

"W-we've got to call the police," Doug said, finally

lowering the gun. It dropped out of his hand and bounced onto the hard ground. I don't think he even noticed.

We all looked like ghosts under the pale fluorescent light. Our skin looked so pale, so ghostly blue.

As if we were *all* dead, I thought.

What a thought.

"We've got to call the police," Doug repeated.

The wind blew the barn door shut again. It slammed noisily, startling us all. Everyone jumped except for the stranger on the floor.

"Maybe the phone is fixed," Red said softly, staring down at the body.

"Go back in the house?" Shannon cried, horrified by the idea.

"We have no choice," Doug said, his voice a choked whisper.

"But, the Jeep—" Shannon started to plead.

"I killed a man. We can't run away," Doug said.

Shannon wrapped her arms around Doug. He really looked as if he were about to collapse or freak out or something.

We heard footsteps behind us, crunching through the frozen snow, then the scraping sound as someone pushed open the barn door. "Lou—" Red cried out, warily taking a few steps away from the corpse, toward the Jeep.

"Thought I heard a gunshot," Lou said, his dark eyes narrowed, staring at us suspiciously. "What are you jokers doing out here in—"

114

He stopped in midsentence when he saw the body on the floor.

"Hey—" he cried, staring at the corpse, blinking, as if he didn't believe what he was seeing.

He ran over to the body and dropped to his knees beside it. "Jake!" he cried. "Hey!" he yelled, staring at me for some reason, his face bright red. "What have you done to Eva's brother?"

chapter
17

"*I*—I shot him," Doug said, his eyes fixed on the revolver at his feet.

"He's dead," Lou said, examining the body, feeling for a pulse in the man's neck. "Jake's dead. I don't believe this."

He searched the corpse's coat pockets and pulled out a blue ski mask. "So Jake was the guy you saw looking in the window," he said bitterly, holding up the ski mask so we could all see it clearly.

Lou's eyes watered over. His face was still bright red. He climbed slowly to his feet, shaking his head. "That's my gun? You killed Jake with *my* gun?"

Lou lunged at Doug. Doug took a step back. For a second it looked as if Lou was going to strangle him.

"Now, wait—" Doug cried, holding up his hands as if to shield himself.

"Don't touch anything," Lou said. "We have to wait

for the police." He looked down at his dead brother-in-law. "Jake," he said, his voice catching in his throat. He swayed unsteadily. I could see that he hadn't sobered up from all the beers he had drunk. Even a grim sight like this couldn't steady him.

He stared angrily at Doug. "Jake was probably coming to help rescue us from this storm."

"I didn't know," Doug said. "I—I didn't mean to shoot. It just went off."

Lou stared at him, scratching his beard with a gloved hand. Then he looked accusingly at Red. "Whose idea was it to steal my gun? What are you suckers doing out here anyway? You stealing my car too? Is that the idea? You fixed my car and didn't tell me. Then you take my gun and my car and leave me and Eva trapped here with a corpse?"

"Now, wait a minute, Lou—" Red started.

But Lou raised his hand to shut Red up. "Put a rag in it, carrot head," he said menacingly. "I can take you. Easy."

Red quickly looked away, trying to avoid a fight.

"I can't believe I let you *murderers* into my house!" Lou cried, cursing and kicking at the wooden post Jake had been leaning against.

"We're not murderers. This was an accident," I said, trying to sound collected, hoping that maybe we could calm Lou down before he went berserk or something.

"Sneaking out in the middle of the night to steal my Jeep was an accident?" Lou screamed, turning his rage on me.

"We have to call the police," I said.

"On what phone?" Lou snapped.

"Then we have to *go* to the police," I said.

"No way," Lou growled. "No way we could make it tonight. The roads have to be sheer ice covered with snow. We'd all end up dead in a ditch somewhere!" He looked down sadly at Eva's brother Jake.

"I'm really sorry," Doug said quietly. "I didn't mean to pull the trigger. I didn't even know I had pulled it."

"We'll go to the police first thing in the morning," Lou said, ignoring Doug. "Get back in the house now. All of you."

"Please—it was an accident!" I cried. He was making me so frightened. He looked so angry.

Lou glared at me. "Red," he said, "give me a hand with Jake. We'll bring him into the house. Down to the cellar. Then I've got to go tell Eva her brother is dead."

Red looked sick. But he grasped Jake's body under the shoulders. Lou grabbed the ankles. They started to carry it from the barn, struggling under the weight. Jake wasn't very big, but all corpses are heavy, I had read.

"Doug—give us a hand," Red called from the barn doorway.

But Doug didn't even hear him. He stood staring at the floor, at the spot where Jake had fallen.

Finally Shannon took Doug's arm and led him to the house. I turned off the light and shoved the barn door shut behind me, and lowering my head against

118

the powerful wind, pressed forward across the dark yard to the kitchen door.

The sprawling house rose in front of me like a prison. We had come so close to getting away. Just a few more yards and we would have been safely inside the Jeep. Just a few more minutes and we would have been out on the road, on our way to the nearest town, to help, to a phone, on our way home.

But now . . .

Who knew what would happen now? Doug had shot a total stranger. Lou had caught us sneaking out, about to steal his only vehicle.

If only we could reach the police tonight, I thought, trying to shiver off the cold as I stepped into the warm kitchen.

"What—what's he going to do with us?" Shannon asked, gripping the arm of my coat.

"I don't know," I said quietly.

"I-I'm so scared. I feel like we'll never get home." Shannon started to tremble.

"Come on," I said, guiding her gently. "We'll go up to my room."

The cellar door was open and we could hear Lou and Red downstairs, struggling with Jake's body. Lou was screaming and cursing.

"I'm frightened too," I said. "We just have to keep out of Lou's way until we can tell our story to the police."

"What will they do to me?" Doug asked, his face red from the cold.

"It was an accident, Doug," I told him. "You didn't

119

deliberately kill Jake. It was a terrible accident. The police will understand."

"They will?" He looked at me hopefully.

"Of course," I said. I didn't really know how the police would react to our story, but I didn't see any reason to get Doug any more upset.

We left our boots by the kitchen door and, carrying our coats, walked up the back stairs to my room. "Here we are again," I said, heaving my coat onto the floor in the corner and gloomily flopping down on the bed.

Doug and Shannon sat down on the rug in front of the radiator, which hissed and spit as it heated the room. We didn't say anything. What was there to say?

Doug rested his arms on his knees, leaned forward, and buried his head. He didn't look up until Red came into the room, his features drawn, his expression frightened.

Red reached down and put a hand on Doug's shoulder. "Hey, listen, man. You're not in this alone, you know."

Doug didn't respond. Red sat down on the edge of the bed near my feet.

"This is all my fault," Red said.

"Come on, Red—" I started.

"No, it's true," he insisted. "I'm the one who told Doug to get the gun. And I'm going to tell the police that. We share the blame. Doug never would have pulled the trigger if I . . ." His voice trailed off. His lower lip trembled. Red struggled to keep control.

"What was that guy Jake doing in the barn?"

Shannon asked so loudly it startled us. She was trembling all over. I wrapped the quilt around her.

"Good question," Red said thoughtfully.

"I mean, if he was the guy in the blue ski mask, why didn't he just come into the house? Why did he poke around outside and then hang out for hours in the barn? And how did he get here if the roads are all closed?"

More good questions. None of us had any answers.

"And why was he carrying a gun?" Doug asked, raking a hand nervously through his black, curly hair.

"Maybe we scared him," Red said, after thinking about it awhile. "Maybe he thought we were thieves or something."

"Which we were," Doug said glumly.

"Lou is the only thief here," Red insisted. "I'm going to tell the police tomorrow. I'm going to tell them that I overheard him plotting with Eva."

"Where *is* Eva?" I asked.

"In her room," Red replied. "Lou went to tell her about her brother. I heard her crying as I passed their room."

Doug uttered a loud cry of anger, of frustration. "It was an accident. Really! I didn't mean to pull the trigger."

Shannon moved over and tried to comfort Doug. I turned to Red. "Those were good questions Shannon was just asking," I said. "I mean, why *was* Jake in that dark, freezing-cold barn with the door shut? And how did he get here?"

Red shrugged.

Other questions started to come to my mind. The whole scene in the barn had happened so quickly. It had been so dark, and then the shot was fired, and we were all so horrified by what had happened, and then the corpse was being carried away, and none of us had had a second to think about it clearly, to question what we had done, what we had been through.

"What are you thinking about, Ariel?" Red asked softly.

"I want to go look at Jake," I said.

"Huh?" His expression turned to surprise. "You want to go downstairs and look at a dead body? Why?"

"Ariel wants to be a doctor," Shannon told him. "Dead bodies don't gross her out like they do normal people." She had her arm around Doug's shoulder. She pressed her face against his, holding him tight, trying to comfort him.

"It all happened so quickly," I said.

"So?"

"Well, I just want to look at it, Red. I mean, why was there so little blood?"

"Blood? There was a little bit of blood," Doug said sadly.

"But just a trickle," I said.

"Hey, you're right," Shannon agreed.

"Maybe it was because it was so cold," Red said. "I mean, maybe his blood froze or something."

"I don't know. Maybe," I said seriously. "Anyway, I'd like to examine the body. Where did you leave it?"

"Don't go down there," Red said, grabbing my arm.

"Please. It'll only upset you. We have to try to keep it together till the police come."

I started to argue with him, but Lou poked his head in the door. "Well, you all look nice and cozy in here," he said bitterly. "Don't anybody move till morning. I'll be right down the hall, and I'll be listening." He pulled the door shut.

Soon after, we tried to sleep a bit, the four of us in our clothes, sprawled about the room. I lay on the bed, wide awake, thinking. Thinking about the corpse. About the gunshot. About the blood.

I had so many questions. I slept a little, but the questions kept waking me up. I knew what I had to do. I had to go see the body.

I looked at my watch. It was a little after six a.m. Silently I pulled on my sneakers. I stopped at the bedroom door and listened in the darkness to make sure no one else was up.

Two lamps were on in the living room, but, peering over the balcony railing, I could see that the room wasn't occupied. In the hall I had heard Lou and Eva talking in their room. Outside, the wind continued to howl. I heard the barn door slam shut. I guess I hadn't closed it very well.

The coast was clear.

I took a deep breath.

Then I crept down the dark stairs and headed for the cellar.

chapter

18

*L*eaning my weight against the banister, I tried to step lightly. But the stairs still creaked and groaned noisily as I made my way down.

I stopped when I reached the back hallway and listened. Silence. No one had heard me.

Outside, I could hear the roar of the wind. There was a loud noise—probably a branch hitting the side of the house. The sound reminded me of the gunshot. I heard the loud explosion again, so near, so terrifyingly near, and saw the man fall to the ground in the darkness.

Shaking my head as if to clear away that memory, I pulled open the doorway to the cellar and searched for a lightswitch. I couldn't find one.

Maybe the light is turned on downstairs, I thought. I waited for my eyes to adjust to the darkness. The steep stairway came into focus. There was no railing to hold on to. I had no choice but to make my way carefully down the stairs in the dark.

I could hear the furnace rumbling in a corner of the cellar. And I heard the steady drip-drip-drip of water somewhere down there—a leaky pipe, most likely.

It got colder as I descended the stairs a step at a time, and the air became heavy and wet. The cellar, obviously, wasn't heated.

I stepped down onto the concrete floor. My sneakers stuck to the damp floor. Everything felt wet and cold and sticky down there. The drip-drip-drip sounded nearer, from somewhere above my head.

Feeling as if I had to sneeze, I held my breath until the sensation passed. I shivered. I wished I had brought my coat.

Feeling blindly along the cold concrete wall, I struggled to find a lightswitch.

"Aagh!"

I couldn't stop myself from uttering a low cry as my hand reached into a thick cobweb. I pulled my hand away quickly and rubbed it against my side, trying to remove the creepy, invisible threads.

"Ohhh."

Now they clung to my face. I closed my eyes and frantically tried to pull them off. I hate cobwebs!

I finally managed to free myself. But now I was itchy all over.

Giving up on finding the lightswitch, I stepped forward, my eyes searching the darkness. Where had they put Jake?

I could still feel the cobweb on my face, even though

I'd removed it. I stopped short, hearing little feet scraping against the concrete floor just in front of me.

Another mouse, probably.

The drip-drip-drip was starting to drive me crazy.

I coughed, the sound echoing deeply, as if I were in an enormous cavern.

In the darkness I could just make out a pile of cardboard cartons against a wall; an old bicycle, one wheel missing, leaning against the cartons; a tall stack of what appeared to be magazines and newspapers; an old couch, one of the cushions missing.

There was a corpse down here somewhere, I knew. I took a few more steps.

And then I thought—what am I doing? Am I really down in a damp, cold cellar searching in the dark for a dead body?

Too late to think about it now, I told myself. You're here. So find Jake and see if you can answer some of your questions.

Having given myself that less than eloquent pep talk, I turned a corner and saw a large canvas tarp stretched out on the floor. Drawing closer, I could see that it bulged up in the center.

I bent down and lifted the tarp, which was heavier than I expected and reeked of mildew. Underneath, on his back, was Jake, lying straight as a board.

I pulled the tarp away, folding it back. Jake stared up at me as if asking, "What are *you* doing here?"

I could barely see him. It was too dark to examine the body. I looked around and finally spotted a light bulb hanging from the ceiling. I walked over to it, felt around until I found a cord, and pulled.

The bulb flicked on. It cast a dim, yellow circle of light onto the cellar floor. It wasn't much, but it would have to do.

Returning to the body, I heard more tiny feet scampering over the concrete. I forced myself not to think about them, not to think about how cold I was, how wet, how frightened.

Be a scientist, Ariel, I told myself. Examine the corpse. Scientifically.

Then run back to your room as fast as your skinny legs will take you!

I bent over Jake's body, my heart pounding.

What should I look at first?

The wound? Yes. The wound.

I pulled open his coat and examined his shirt. The bullet had entered just above his stomach in the center of his rib cage. The front of the shirt had a gaping hole in it to match the one in his coat, as if a giant had grabbed hold of the material and pulled off a big piece of it. The flannel was burned and frayed. The opening was as big as a cannonball.

Leaning close, struggling to see in the dim light, I examined the wound. It was much smaller than the hole in the shirt.

And just as I had remembered, there was practically no blood. A small amount had clotted around the circle of the wound. But the shirt wasn't soaked with blood, and no blood had run down the chest.

Interesting, I thought.

Really interesting.

I had a hunch now, an idea of what was going on here.

But I had to make sure.

I backed up a bit, shifted my position, and picked up the corpse's hand.

It was stiff and frozen.

Ice cold.

I dropped it back to the floor. The entire arm was stiff.

I felt the arm. I felt a shoulder. Frozen.

I looked at my watch, holding it up to read it in the dim yellow light. It was six-thirty. That meant that Doug had shot Jake less than six hours ago.

I guessed that a body couldn't get this stiff in that much time. No way.

So why was Jake's body completely frozen?

It wasn't cold enough for a body to freeze in this cellar. That meant that—

Footsteps.

I jumped to my feet.

Shoes clomped on the concrete floor.

Someone was in the basement with me.

chapter
19

"Who—who is it?" I called softly.

My voice echoed off the concrete walls.

I heard the drip-drip-drip of the leaky pipe. And I heard the footsteps grow louder.

I held my breath and turned around.

Red stepped into the light.

He squinted at me, as if trying to focus, trying to wake up. His red hair was sticking out every which way. His sneakers were untied.

"Ariel?"

"Red—I'm so glad it's you!" I cried. I was so relieved, I wanted to run up and hug him.

"I had a feeling I'd find you down here," he said, rubbing the sleeves of his sweatshirt. "Man, it's cold."

"I—I had to see some things," I said.

"It sure smells down here." He looked down at the

129

body. "Want me to help you cover it up?" He started toward the canvas tarp.

"No. Let's just get back upstairs," I said, hurrying over to him. "Are Doug and Shannon up?"

"Yeah. I think so," he said, yawning and stretching. "I don't know. I'm not really awake yet myself. Didn't sleep too well."

"I didn't either," I said. I took his hand and pulled him toward the stairs. "Come on. Hurry. We've all got to talk."

"Why? What did you find down here?"

"I'll tell you upstairs," I said.

Doug and Shannon appeared to be very tired and confused as Red and I crept back into my room. "What's up?" Shannon asked, trying to straighten her coppery hair with one hand.

"A lot," I said.

I closed the door behind us and started to tell them what I had learned down in the cellar. "We're being set up," I said. "Doug, you didn't kill Jake."

"Huh?" Red cried.

Doug's face filled with confusion. "But I shot him, Ariel."

"Yes, you shot him," I agreed. "But Jake was already dead!"

"That's crazy!" Red cried. "Why do you say that?"

"Because Jake didn't bleed," I said. "Only a trickle. If he'd been alive, the blood would have gushed. And when I examined him just now, he was stiff. Much too stiff to be dead for such a short time."

"But—" Doug started.

"And his body was ice cold. Nearly frozen. He must have been in the barn for quite a while. Dead. That's the only way his body would be frozen like that."

"But he was standing right in front of us!" Shannon protested. "We all saw him."

"He wasn't standing," I said, seeing it very clearly in my mind. "He was leaning. Leaning against that post. He must have been propped up there. Propped up with the gun jammed into his hand."

"Now, wait a minute, Ariel. How do you figure that?" Red asked, glancing up from tying his sneakers.

"Because when Doug shot him, his body didn't resist at all. He didn't cry out, or fall forward, or anything. The bullet sent him flying backward, right? He fell so stiffly. If it hadn't been so dark, if we hadn't been so scared, we would have noticed it right away."

"Ariel is right," Doug said, staring into my eyes, thinking hard. "Of course she's right. But why—"

"It's a set-up," I said, whispering loudly, excitedly. "Lou has set us up. Don't you see? He probably murdered Jake and then decided to pin it on us."

"You mean—" Doug started.

"I mean that Lou's idea is to take us to the police and have you confess to shooting Jake. You *did* shoot him, after all. The local police won't question it. They probably won't even examine the body that closely to find out how Jake was *really* killed. They'll have your confession, after all. They'll have the gun. They'll see the bullet wound. So that will be that. Lou gets off scot-free, and we—we—"

"I think you're jumping to a lot of conclusions," Red said quietly. "I just can't accept the idea that—"

"Ariel is right!" Doug repeated. "Of *course* she's right. This whole thing was a trap! Jake was already dead. And we were so stupid, we just—"

"Doug, you just want to get off the hook," Red insisted.

"Stop it. Stop arguing!" Shannon cried.

"Shannon's right," I said. "There's no time. We've got to get out of here." I pulled on my coat and picked up my bag. "If I'm right, Lou has already killed once. And we're the only ones who know about it."

What was to keep Lou from killing again, from killing all four of us so that his secret would be safe?

I suddenly found myself thinking about Eva. Did she know that Lou had killed Jake? Did she know his bizarre plan for making it look as if *we* were the killers? Was she in on the plan?

She must be, I decided. Eva must know.

Both of them were dangerous. Both of them were murderers.

"I think we should stay and confront Lou," Red said, blocking the doorway to my room. "I mean, what's the point of running away now? If we run, it's just going to make us look guilty."

"We're not running away," I said. "We're running right to the police. And we're going to tell them everything we know—before Lou can make it look like he's an innocent victim and we barged into his house, accepted his hospitality, and murdered his brother-in-law!"

"But how will we get away?" Red asked, looking both ways down the hall, as if he heard Lou or Eva approaching.

"We'll take the Jeep, of course," I said. "You have the keys, right, Red?"

He nodded. "I still don't think—"

Red looked really frightened. I figured he was afraid of what Lou would do to us if he caught us trying to escape a second time.

"We have no choice, Red," I said, attempting to push past him. "We have to get out of here. *Now*. Come on."

Reluctantly he stepped out of the way. I didn't blame him for being scared. Now that we knew Lou was a murderer and not just a loud-mouthed, macho show-off, the situation was even scarier than it had seemed.

But I knew I was right. I knew we had to get away.

This time we didn't sneak down the back stairs. We *ran*.

I led the way, followed by Doug and Shannon, and then Red.

There was no sign of Lou or Eva. I hoped they were asleep. Our running down the stairs was sure to wake them up. But we'd be long gone by the time Lou could get dressed and come after us.

We frantically pulled on our boots, then ran out the

back door. An instant later we were running across the ice-encrusted snow, balancing our packs and bags as we ran toward the barn.

A big orange sun was just coming up behind us. It made the snow sparkle like gold. Our shadows were long and bright blue. The wind had died down. The whole world looked bright and clean. But I was too scared to enjoy the beauty of the morning.

I just wanted to get to that Jeep, to drive far away from this house and never see it again.

We were nearly to the barn when I turned back to Doug and Shannon. "Hey—where's Red?"

All three of us stopped and turned around.

"He was right behind us," Doug said, breathing heavily.

"Is he still in the house?" Shannon asked.

I shielded my eyes with my hand and stared back at the house. The kitchen door swung open, and I saw Red come running toward us, slipping and sliding as he made his way quickly over the icy snow.

He was waving something in his hand. Something that caught the morning sun and reflected its light.

As he ran closer, I saw what it was. A pistol.

"Hey—" I yelled. "Throw it away!"

He paid no attention. Just kept running full speed over the snow. I wasn't sure he had heard me.

"Throw it away, Red!" I shouted. "We don't need that!"

"I do!" Red said, stopping a few yards in front of us, his breath forming white clouds that drifted up toward the sky. He raised the small silver pistol and pointed it at me.

"Sorry," Red said, squinting against the bright light reflected off the snow. "You're nice guys. But Lou and I worked too hard to set this whole thing up. I can't let you go now."

chapter
20

*T*he three of us were too shocked to say anything. I just stared at Red, at the pistol in his hand, the pistol pointed at me.

"This is a joke—right?" I said finally.

He shook his head no. He gestured toward the house with the gun.

"You mean you're working with Lou?" Doug asked, his voice rising in disbelief. "You brought us here deliberately?"

"You're catching on, Doug," Red said flatly. His face was expressionless, but he kept his eyes trained on me. "You might say I recruited you guys. At the ski lodge."

The ski lodge. That seemed such a long time ago.

"But you can't get away with this!" Shannon cried, grabbing on to Doug's arm.

Red didn't reply. He glanced back at the house and then gestured with the pistol again. "Come on, guys. Let's go. We've got a schedule to keep."

He walked behind us, the pistol poised, as we slowly trudged back toward the house. No one said a word. The only sound was the crunching of our boots on the hard snow.

I felt like such an idiot.

How could I have trusted Red?

How could I have been *attracted* to him?

He had fooled me completely. Fooled all of us. We had trusted him. We had thanked him for saving our lives.

And the whole time he was laughing at us, guiding us into the trap that he and Lou were setting up.

I felt so angry, and so hurt, and so totally betrayed.

But there was nothing to do but march back up to the house and see what new terrors Red and Lou and Eva had in store for us.

The surface of the snow was so ice-laden and hard, we could practically walk on top of it. Red made us stop just outside the kitchen door. He kept the gun trained on us and shouted for Lou.

Lou appeared almost immediately, as if he'd been waiting by the door. He was wearing his baggy jeans and a tan hunting jacket.

"Good morning, gang," he said, grinning for some reason.

"Here you go," Red said and flipped the pistol to Lou.

Lou stepped out onto the small stoop, turning the pistol in his hand until he had it pointed at us. "Hey, the wind is gone," he said, surveying the backyard. "Nice morning, huh?"

We didn't reply. All three of us were keeping our eyes on the pistol.

"Now where were you turkeys going on such a nice morning?" Lou asked, his smile fading. "You weren't trying to sneak away again, were you?"

He didn't really expect an answer, so we didn't give one.

"You wouldn't try running away after killing Eva's brother, would you? Poor old Jake. We've got to tell the police about Jake, right? Isn't that what we decided?"

A big clump of snow fell off the roof beside Lou. The noise startled him momentarily. He recovered quickly and jumped off the top step of the stoop into the snow, keeping the gun trained on us.

"The phone is fixed, gang. Isn't that good news? So we can call the police and you can make your confession."

"We know the truth, Lou," I said, unable to hold myself in any longer.

He stared at me. "The truth?"

"We know Doug didn't kill Jake. We know Jake was already dead."

Lou turned to Red. "What did you bring me here, pal? These kids are too smart."

Red shrugged. He had his hands stuffed in his jeans

pockets. He was standing off to the side, as if watching the show.

"Too smart," Lou repeated, his expression now menacing. He stared at me. "So you've figured out everything, huh? You've even figured out that Red was the one wearing the blue ski mask. All of our secrets. You're just too smart. Too smart to live, maybe." He scratched his beard thoughtfully.

"What are we going to do, Lou?" Red asked, looking at the barn. The door was stuck open, wedged in the snow. I could just make out the Jeep against the far wall, deep in shadow.

"Let's think," Lou said. "We've got to get our story straight. These kids aren't our only problem right now."

"What do you mean?" Red snapped, a worried expression tightening his features.

"It's Eva," Lou said. "She's giving me trouble. She promised to cooperate. But now she's acting like a baby."

A crow eased down onto the snow a few yards behind us, cawing loudly, flapping its wings, black against the white snow. Lou aimed the pistol at it and pretended to shoot it, making shooting noises with his mouth.

"Eva's upset about Jake?" Red asked.

Lou nodded, frowning. "Yeah. Can you imagine? At this late date Eva decides she loved her brother."

"He was my brother too," Red said with some emotion.

So—Red was Eva's brother!

"You're not changing your mind too?" Lou snapped angrily.

"No. No," Red protested, his eyes widening in fear. "I understand why you killed him, Lou. Eva has to understand too."

"I'm sorry," said a voice from the doorway. Eva stepped out, her hair unbrushed, in tangles about her head, her eyes wild and frightened.

"Eva, get back in the house," Lou said quietly but forcefully.

She ignored him. Her eyes darted over to us. She seemed almost surprised to see us standing there. Then she turned back to her husband.

"I can't go through with it, Lou," she said, her voice trembling. "I'm sorry. I thought I could. But I just can't."

"Eva—get back in the house," Lou repeated in a low growl, obviously struggling not to lose his temper.

"I hated Jake for what he did to us," Eva continued, clasping the top of her open coat and pulling it closed around her neck. "Jake was detestable. Stealing our inheritance over the years, cheating us of what was rightfully ours."

"Eva," Lou growled, losing his patience. "We don't have to go into ancient history now, do we? Please—"

"But you didn't have to kill him, Lou," Eva interrupted, ignoring him, staring out at the frozen lake behind the barn. "I—I just can't go through with this. I'm sorry."

"It's too late to be sorry," Lou said, scowling.

"I called the police," Eva told him. "They're on their way. They'll be here in twenty minutes, maybe less."

My heart jumped.

Those were the best words I'd heard in a long time.

I glanced over at Shannon without moving my head. She returned the glance. I could see she was as happy as I was.

Lou, of course, had a different reaction.

"Are you crazy?" he screamed at Eva, his face reddening. He swore and gestured with the pistol, waving it angrily at us. "You know, you're not one of *them*, Eva. You're not an innocent bystander here. You're in this too, Babe. You're in it up to your pretty neck!"

Twenty minutes, I thought.

They'll be here in twenty minutes.

That's too long. We're not out of danger yet.

A lot can happen in twenty minutes.

"I don't believe you called the police, Eva," Red said, obviously very frightened. He wiped his forehead with the sleeve of his coat. He was perspiring despite the cold.

Lou and Eva started to argue loudly, ignoring Doug, Shannon, and me completely.

I looked down on the ground and something struck my eye. It was the stockpile of snowballs Doug had made during our snowball fight the morning before.

They must be hard as ice, I thought.

Lou had his back to us now, as he continued cursing and screaming at Eva. Red moved toward the stoop to join in the argument.

It seemed like the perfect time. The *only* time.

I had to try.

I bent down quickly, grabbed up two of the ice-hard snowballs and heaved one of them at Lou's head.

chapter

21

My first snowball missed by at least a foot.

It smacked against the back of the house, making a loud clap.

Lou jumped at the sound and turned away from Eva. Then he glared at Doug, fear mixed with anger on his face.

And that's when I let my second snowball go.

Again, I threw without aiming. There wasn't time, and I was too scared anyway. My heart pounding in my chest, the sparkling white ground seeming to tilt and spin before my eyes.

I threw with all my strength, all my anger, all my frustration.

Bull's-eye!

My second snowball smacked Lou right in the forehead.

It was rock hard. It stunned him.

He cried out, his eyes closing in pain and surprise.

The force of the throw made him stagger back against the low stoop.

The silver pistol dropped from his hand into the snow.

Now everything seemed to move in slow motion.

Still sitting back awkwardly against the stoop, Lou cursed and grabbed his forehead. Small clumps of snow and ice dripped down his cheeks, along his beard.

Eva, above him on the stoop, stood rigid, staring at Lou, confused, appearing not to understand what had just happened.

No one moved.

It seemed as if time itself had frozen. As if we all had frozen.

And then everyone moved at once.

Red dived for the gun, leaping into the snow, thrusting both arms forward.

Doug dived a second later.

Red almost had his hand on the pistol.

But Doug tackled him hard, pushing him away. Red grabbed desperately for the gun—and missed.

Doug jumped on top of him and, with a loud cry, like the desperate roar of a wild animal, grabbed the back of Red's head and shoved his face hard into the snow.

Then, still on top of Red, Doug reached down into the snow, grabbed the pistol, pulled his arm back— and tossed it across the yard.

I didn't wait to see it land.

Without a word to each other, Shannon and I started running, running toward the barn. I don't know what I had in mind. I don't think I had anything in mind—just escape.

To get away from that house.

I turned around and saw that Doug was right behind us, running hard over the snow. "The Jeep! The Jeep!" he was shouting.

Red, Lou, and Eva were screaming at one another in front of the stoop.

Where was the pistol? I wondered.

Hadn't anyone retrieved the gun?

"The Jeep! The Jeep!" Doug kept shouting wildly, motioning us forward with both arms.

He didn't have to motion us. Shannon and I were running as fast as we could.

I ducked, my head low, and leaned forward as I ran. I kept expecting to hear the crack of the pistol.

I'm going to be shot, I thought. Shot in the back.

Shannon slipped and uttered a short cry as she fell. She landed on her knees, then lifted herself quickly with her arms.

I reached back and grabbed her hand. I started pulling her toward the barn.

"The Jeep! The Jeep!" Doug kept shouting.

Where were Red and Lou? Were they coming after us? Had they found the pistol?

Were they still arguing with Eva?

Were they *letting* us get away?

145

I didn't look back. I just ran, gasping for air, my boots crunching over the hard, slick snow.

A few seconds later we were in the barn. Blinking in the sudden darkness, I was the first one to the Jeep. I flung open the passenger door and climbed into the back.

Breathing hard, her face revealing her terror, Shannon lifted herself into the passenger seat.

Doug pulled open the door to the driver's seat. He started to climb in.

Then he stopped.

All of the color drained from his face.

"Doug—what's the matter? Get in!" I shouted.

"What are we thinking of?" he cried. "How can we be so stupid?" He lowered himself back to the ground. "Red has the keys!"

chapter

22

 Trapped.

Cornered.

I was stunned by how stupid we had been, too stunned to utter a cry.

The barn had suddenly become a prison.

In our panic to escape we had run into an even worse trap.

Shannon and I climbed out of the Jeep. I could see Lou and Red running toward us from the house, shouting as they approached the barn.

"There's got to be another way out!" Shannon cried.

"There's no back door," Doug said. "There's not even a window."

There was no escape.

Or was there?

Looking around desperately, my eyes fell on the

snowmobile leaning against the back wall. I ran over to it, surprised to see that it was just like the ones I had ridden during our family's last winter vacation.

Would it run?

Lou had said it hadn't worked in years.

But he and Red most likely had lied about the Jeep being broken. Maybe Lou had lied about the snowmobile too.

It's got to work, *got* to work, I told myself, glancing out the door.

They were less than a hundred yards from the barn, running fast, shouting angrily.

I decided it was worth a try.

I mean, what did we have to lose?

There wasn't time to say anything to Doug and Shannon, who had started to look for a place to hide. But except for the stack of cartons in one corner, the barn was almost empty, completely open.

No place to hide.

It's *got* to work, *got* to work, I kept repeating.

The snowmobile had a pull-rope to start it, like a power lawn mower.

Hoping against hope, I grabbed it with both hands and tugged.

To my surprise, the snowmobile immediately roared to life.

"It works!" I shouted.

Doug and Shannon spun around in surprise as I pulled the snowmobile away from the wall and climbed on. "Maybe I can make 'em chase me!" I shouted over the roar of the engine. "Then you can run for help down on the road!"

They looked confused.

"Run to the road!" I shouted. "To the road! Get help! Get the police! Just run!"

I wasn't sure if they had heard me or not.

But there was no time to find out.

I looked up to see Lou and Red in the doorway to the barn.

Did they have the gun?

I couldn't tell.

They stood side by side, blocking the door.

I gunned the engine, aimed the snowmobile right at them, and roared forward.

chapter
23

*T*he noise of the engine was deafening.

Lou and Red were silhouettes in the doorway against the white snow outside. I aimed the snowmobile right at Lou.

I couldn't hear what he and Red were shouting. But I saw their eyes go wide as I roared up to them. And then I saw them dive to the side just as I reached the door.

Then I was out, out in the snow.

The blinding white light made me close my eyes. I opened them and squinted against the glare.

I was sliding easily over the slick snow, heading away from the barn, away from the house, toward the ice-covered lake.

Had Shannon and Doug escaped from the barn? Not yet.

Lou and Red were struggling to their feet and heading in my direction!

What luck! Somehow my scheme had worked!

Now. Go now. I silently urged Doug and Shannon.

I spun back toward the lake, almost turning the thing on its side, and opened it up full throttle.

If only I could keep the two of them busy chasing me until the police arrived.

If the police arrived.

If the police were on their way.

The thought suddenly flashed through my mind that Eva may not have been telling the truth about calling the police. Maybe she had just been threatening Lou, or trying to see how he'd react.

Maybe the police weren't coming at all.

I was nearly to the lake. It stretched in front of me.

I looked back. Lou and Red were running hard. Despite the fact that I was riding and they were on foot, they didn't seem that far behind me!

Kicking up a high spray of snow, the snowmobile slid onto the icy lake. Where the snow had been blown off, I could see that the ice near the shore was solid white and hard. But as I roared straight ahead, I saw patches of uncovered dark ice. That meant it wasn't entirely frozen in those places.

I knew I had to stay on the solid white ice. The snowmobile was heavy. If I drove onto a spot where the ice was weak, I was sure to crack the ice and plummet into the freezing water underneath.

I wondered if Shannon and Doug had sneaked out

to the road. I wondered if they were going to find someone to help us.

Lou and Red were at the edge of the lake, and coming on fast, running a few steps, then sliding on the slick surface. Running, then sliding.

Just ahead I noticed a large dark patch of ice. I swerved to avoid it—

And started to tilt.

I could feel the snowmobile go out of control. And I had this sick feeling of helplessness, of knowing what was about to happen, of not being able to do anything but let it happen.

I guess I'd been going too fast, or tried to turn too sharply on the smooth surface.

With a grinding roar, the snowmobile bolted over onto its side. I let go and went flying off it, landing hard on my side on the ice.

I let out one gasp and then realized I couldn't breathe.

I had had the wind knocked out of me.

In a total panic, unable to move, unable to get up, struggling to take air into my lungs, I watched the snowmobile slide away from me.

Get up, Ariel. Get up.

Breathe.

You've got to breathe now.

The white snow looked so blue. Everything looked blue.

Was I staring up at the sky?

Had the whole world turned upside down?

Breathe, Ariel. Come on, girl—breathe!

I could hear Lou's voice, shouting and cursing. I think it snapped me out of my daze, out of my pain.

I gulped in a mouthful of air. Then another.

I was on my feet now. The snowmobile had come to a stop on its side at the edge of the dark patch of ice. Useless to me now.

Red and Lou were just a few yards behind me. Running and sliding.

I tried to run, too, but the snow was so deep and the lake surface so slick, so slippery. My boots couldn't take hold. I could barely walk.

Looking back toward the house, I saw Doug and Shannon running toward the lake.

Alone.

Why were they running back?

To help me, I guessed. They must have seen that I was in trouble and were running to the lake to try to help.

"Stop right there!" Lou shouted, his voice echoing off the hard surface.

"Stop, Ariel! You can't get away!" Red cried, right behind him.

They were probably right. They were close behind me and gaining.

It was just so hard to run through the snow on the ice.

No, no, no, I thought.

I had been running so long, scared so long, trying to get away from them for so long that I was panting, my chest heaving, gasping out loud with each breath.

I felt as if my lungs were about to burst. My legs

153

throbbed. My ribs ached from my fall off the snowmobile.

No, no, no.

I kept running. To the edge of a patch of dark ice.

And then I slipped and fell forward, sprawling onto my stomach.

"Gotcha," Lou said in a low voice, right behind me.

chapter
24

*L*ou reached out both hands and grabbed my legs. I kicked furiously, sending up a shower of snow and toppling him backward.

Before I could get up, Red grabbed my shoulders and pushed me down, pinning me in place.

"Ow! Stop! Get off me!"

Were they going to kill me right there in the middle of the lake?

Lou got up quickly and stood over me, glaring angrily, breathing hard.

"Let go of me!" I struggled to get free of Red, but he leaned all of his weight on me, holding me in place.

"Now what?" Red asked, glancing up at Lou.

Lou was about to answer when we heard the sirens in the distance.

"Huh?" Red's expression changed as fear mingled with surprise on his face.

"Eva really did it," Lou muttered grimly. "She called the police." He cursed under his breath.

Red jumped to his feet, forgetting about me. The sirens grew louder. "Now what?" Red repeated. "Now what, Lou? Now what, Genius? Mr. *Plans?* What's the big plan now, Genius?!" He said the word with total disgust, his voice high-pitched, almost hysterical.

"Shut up!" Lou snarled, balling up his fist as if he were about to hit Red.

I slid away from them, afraid to get up, glad not to be noticed for a few seconds.

I edged slowly, silently away from Red and Lou.

The sirens were really close now.

"Now what? Now what?" Red repeated, his voice frightened and cracking.

"Shut up. Let me think," Lou said, scratching his beard.

"We're trapped!" Red cried. "Trapped! All because of you and your stupid plan, Lou."

"Shut up, Red. I mean it."

I edged my way farther out on the lake, praying their argument would continue, that they wouldn't notice me until I was far from them.

"I *knew* it wouldn't work!" Red screamed, giving Lou a hard shove. "You always have to make things complicated. We should've killed Jake and then taken off. That's simple enough."

"*You're* simple," Lou growled. "Everyone in this little town knew we were visiting Jake. When he turned up dead, the police would've come after us. We never could've gotten the money back that Jake stole.

Staying here and bringing these kids in to blame—
that was smart," Lou said.

"We should've buried him and run," Red insisted.

I edged my way farther out. I climbed to my feet and
started to move, half running, half sliding over the ice.

"Buried him where? Where should we have buried
him? In the snow?" Lou screamed. "You're as dumb
as your sister!"

"Well, look where your brilliant plan got us!" Red
screamed hysterically. "We're trapped here. Caught
with nowhere to run."

"Come on, Red—" Lou's expression turned sor-
rowful.

The sirens were blaring now. The police must have
been at the front of the house. Doug and Shannon
were at the edge of the lake.

"Well, I'm not gonna be a sitting duck!" Red
screamed. "You can stand here and surrender, Lou.
I'm gonna grab the girl." He looked at me, his eyes
wild and frightened. "They're not taking me—unless
they want to see her dead!"

chapter

25

I could feel my heart leap.

My breath caught in my throat.

What was taking the police so long?

Looking up at the house, I saw Eva running toward the lake, her coat undone, flapping wildly behind her.

But no police cars.

Red started toward me, his face grim, determined.

I started to run again, slipping, sliding, struggling to keep my balance.

"Hey!" he yelled. "Stop!"

Everything was so white, so shiny. Even in my terror I saw once again that white sheet of paper my dad used to hold up and make jokes about.

"What do you see here, Ariel?"

"A frightened girl who might die in the snow."

Some joke.

I ran blindly into the white glare, sliding, tumbling forward as if in a dream, a terrifying, cold, white nightmare. All color disappeared. I was hurtling through an all-white world, so sparkling clear, so . . . dangerously clear.

The colors returned as Red lunged at me, groaning as he threw his arms out.

I dodged to one side, ducking my head.

He missed me and kept moving.

He was going so fast, I didn't think he could stop himself.

And then I heard the cracking, the mysterious cracking.

Like bones breaking.

I looked down, but couldn't see anything through the snow.

Then when Red screamed, I turned back to him. And heard the ice shattering under him.

The cracking noise was so loud, like someone tearing apart the earth.

Red raised his arms. I'll never forget the look of horror on his face. His mouth was open wide. His frightened eyes staring straight up for some reason.

"Ariel—"

I think I heard him call my name.

And then he dropped through the snow and ice.

It didn't look as if he were falling. He went down so fast, it looked as if he were being *sucked* down.

I stood there, watching, unable to move, to do anything.

I saw his horrified face. The expression didn't change as it disappeared into the dark water. His hands, held high above his head, vanished last.

"Red! Red! Red!"

I could hear Eva shrieking his name over and over from the edge of the lake.

Red struggled up to the surface.

His arms were flailing frantically.

He looked like the little mouse in the trap.

"Red! Red! Red!"

He reached a hand toward me.

I edged forward, listening for the ice to crack again. A bit more. A bit more.

"Red! Red! Red!"

I reached my hand out, leaning forward, stretching as far as I could.

Could I get to him before the ice broke? Before he sank again?

I was only a few feet from him now.

And then only a foot away.

Lying down, I stretched—stretched toward him—stretched. . . .

And the ice cracked loudly, a big chunk breaking away.

I jumped back. Just in time.

Red rolled over in the water, pushed by the heavy, broken chunks of ice.

"Red! Red! Red!"

He disappeared headfirst under the snow and ice.

He didn't surface again.

I lay staring at the hole, at the dark water that

splashed up over the edges. I don't know how long I lay there, waiting for Red to pop back up.

But I knew.

I knew Red was dead.

I suddenly realized that I was pulling at my hair with both hands. Standing up, I took a step back. Then another.

Eva was still screaming Red's name from the shore. Lou was hurrying across the ice to her.

A loud crack startled me.

The ice beneath my boots—it was starting to break up.

"Ohhh!"

I suddenly realized that I was about to be sucked down under the ice like Red.

chapter

26

I took another careful step toward the shore.

I couldn't decide whether to work my way slowly step by step or to run as fast as I could and hope that I could outrun the shattering ice.

I heard another crack, nearby.

Water sprung up and splashed over my boots.

I tried to erase Red's horrified face from my mind. But it refused to go away.

I saw his face, saw his hand reach for mine, heard Eva's heartbreaking shrieks.

Stop thinking, Ariel, I told myself. Just get yourself back onto solid ground.

I looked to the shore, so close yet so far away. Standing on the edge of the lake, Lou was doing his best to comfort Eva.

Behind them, two black-and-white police cars skidded into the backyard, the flashing red lights on their roofs reflecting pink off the snow.

Finally! I thought.

I took another step, waving to the police cars.

I was too frightened to call out to them, frightened that a loud noise might make the ice crack even more. I know that's not scientific. But it's hard to be scientific when you're scared out of your wits!

Doug and Shannon were waving and calling to the policemen, who came leaping out of their cars, their guns drawn.

Lou quickly surrendered. He had his arms around Eva. He didn't try to escape.

Everyone was standing on the lakeshore staring across the ice at me now.

"Run, Ariel! It's going to give way!" Doug shouted. He held his hands out to me.

The cracking suddenly sounded like thunder, the kind of thunder that starts quietly in the distance and then becomes a roar as it moves toward you.

I didn't turn back to see how close the open water was to me.

I followed Doug's advice. I started to run.

I was almost there, just a few yards from Doug's outstretched hands.

Another crack, again like thunder.

I could feel the ice breaking up.

I'm not going to make it. I'm not going to make it.

I *am* going to make it!

I reached forward and grabbed Doug's hands.

He pulled me onto land just as I felt the entire

section beneath my feet give way. I looked back and saw chunks of ice bobbing and swaying, like gigantic ice cubes in an enormous drink.

I smiled at Doug, holding on to his shoulders. "Nice catch," I said.

"I can't believe we'll be home by dinner time," Shannon said.

"Yeah. I wonder what's for dinner," Doug said, his eyes staring straight ahead through the windshield. "Hope it isn't liver."

"I'm sure my parents will wait to ask *me* what to have tonight," I said, laughing. "Mom was so happy to hear from me, I think she and Dad will be my slaves for at least the next year or two!"

"Yeah, my parents were so relieved, they forgot how angry they are at me," Shannon added.

We'd been driving for more than an hour and she hadn't complained about the broken heater once. I didn't think any of us would complain about *anything* —not for a long while, anyway.

We were that grateful to be heading home.

The police had arrested Lou and Eva. They took us all to the police station, where they let us call our parents. Mom and Dad were both home, waiting by the phone. They'd been up for two days, worried sick. They had tried to call, but of course the lines were down. They seemed so glad to hear my voice, and I *know* I'd never been so glad to hear theirs!

After the phone calls the town police captain called

us one by one into his tiny closet of an office to tell the whole story in detail.

Then Doug's Plymouth had to be towed out of the ravine. That took nearly two hours. The passenger side was pretty bent up. The front door wouldn't even open. But—miracle of miracles—the engine started right up! It was weird to think that it was Red who had pushed the car into the ravine.

And finally, here we were, on our way to our homes in Shadyside. "I don't believe it," Doug had said, leaning forward. "The road's been plowed!"

"The road crew waited until it was time for us to leave," Shannon said, resting her head against the seatback.

"Hey—what are you guys doing *next* weekend?" I asked, leaning forward between the front seats.

"I don't know. Why?" Shannon asked.

"How about a ski weekend?" I suggested, laughing.

Doug and Shannon didn't think it was funny.

"I have something for you," Doug said, seriously. With his left hand on the wheel, he reached over, opened the glove compartment, and pulled out a snowball. Without taking his eyes off the road, he reached back and rubbed it in my face.

I guess I deserved it.

I decided I'd get him back the first time we stopped.

About the Author

R. L. STINE is the author of more than a dozen mysteries and thrillers for Young Adult readers. He also writes funny novels and joke books.

In addition to his publishing work, he is Head Writer of the children's TV show "Eureeka's Castle." And he is Editorial Director of *Nickelodeon* magazine.

He lives in New York City with his wife, Jane, and son, Matt.

WATCH OUT FOR

THE FIRE GAME

(Coming in March 1991)

At first it was a joke. Set a small fire
and miss the geography test. But before long,
Jill and her friends are into the excitement
of the fire game. It's all because of Gabe,
the handsome new kid in town who taunts
them, dares them—until what starts out as a
game—ends in a murder!